THE FOLLOWERS PART TWO

THE DEVILS BONE

This is a work of fiction. All of the characters, organizations, and events portrayed in this Novel are either products of the Author's imaginations, or are used fictitiously.

ISBN: 13978-0692955413

This book is dedicated to my children, Tiffany, Michael, Desiree, and Katie.

May the sun always shine on you, in all you do.

To my granddaughter Angel, my painting partner,

may all your dreams come true

The albino ran through the alley seeking the comfort of the darkness. He was injured and blood dripped from his shoulder and leg. Pain was new to him. He was usually the one dispensing it. He wanted revenge, to tear the man who shot him in half.

Finally, groaning he eased himself onto the ground, next to a large dumpster.

The darkness engulfed him. He couldn't run another step. Nathan, as he had been called in another life, pushed the button that dangled on the leather string hanging around his neck.

He didn't quite grasp it, but he knew once he activated it, they would find him and make him better. That's what the priestess had said. She made him repeat it back, to ensure that he understood. Nathan trusted her. Anita was all he had.

He had been abandoned by his parents, and grown up in an orphanage. It was a run- down hole in the wall, with little food, and daily beatings and ridicule.

Before he had been abandoned his mother, a prostitute, had loaned him out to the highest bidder whenever times got rough. The men did what they wanted and paid good money for it.

As he became older, and larger, he became a burden, a freak show, so to speak. When he turned ten he was the size of a grown man. He was now a liability to his mother and her customers. Letha had dropped him off in front of the orphanage, screeching off in her Cadillac.

Nathan had stood on the sidewalk and starred at the ominous looking two story house, with its cracked stucco, and broken shades.

Finally near dark he was ushered inside. The other children pointed and laughed. He was a pink eyed, white creature, that didn't fit in. From the beginning, they poked and prodded him. He was laughed at, and beaten. It became a weekly ritual. Nathan took every beating, every ridicule, and turned it to hate.

That hate festered for years. He left the orphanage at 18, and within a week he killed his first prostitute.

It made him feel full inside. It stifled the hate for a short time. Anita snagged him up a few weeks later. She had been watching him. He was slow and easily manipulated.

His size was a plus due to the intimidation factor. Through him she controlled others. The cult was disbanded, and she had to work hard to recruit new members. The elders feared him, and with him at her side she would always have the upper hand.

Now that Megan and Mark were back together, and she had to hide to keep from going to jail, it had taken a long time for her supporters to put money back into the church.

The press had called it a Cult, but to Anita it would always be the Church of the Divine Rainbow. It had been practiced by her father, and his father before him.

Granted in the last years her father had gone semi mad, and the new traditions began. To Anita it was law. She would do anything she could to uphold it.

After the bombing the publicity had been too much. Most of the high ranking officials that had not been charged or exposed were lying low, and funding was slim. The lower members dead, silenced forever.

Anita had high hopes that she would rebuild, and all would not be lost. After all she had the greatest trump card of all. She had the one thing that she had always wanted. The gold prize everyone was looking for.

Well, truth be told, she thought they probably weren't even looking anymore.

The heat had died down, and they had the other baby after all. Megan had, had ample opportunity to join her, and had decided to run off with that man instead.

The elders had been disappointed, since they were looking forward to the ascension, as much as she was. Everything had changed, and she had to convince them that the baby was also a direct, pure descendant, of the bloodline.

Four hours later the black cargo van pulled up next to the dumpster.

Nathan had passed out an hour before. It took 3 men to load the massive monstrosity into the back.

George called the number that had been provided to him.

"Yes?" the voice at the other end answered. "We have him."

"And the house?"

"Compromised, crawling with Feds."

"Where is the girl?"

"Gone." There was silence at the other end.

"Ma'am?"

"Bring Nathan back to me."

"Yes Ma'am."

"Did you get the new ID Made for him?"

"Yes Ma'am, just like you asked. He is now "Francis Smith.""

"Good, I don't want the feds catching up with him if he does ever get out in public, and George, I'm going to have a very special assignment for you when you return."

"Whatever you need." He hung up and looked at the sleeping figure in the back.

"Let's go, he's out." George said to Ray, a little Cuban man, he had picked up to help him. He damn sure couldn't carry the big bastard by himself.

George was a tall wiry man, thin, with beady blue eyes, and short cut blond hair.

He looked nervous, always running back and forth, his eyes shifting around. He was always moving. Watching him made people nervous.

He was one of those pacers, someone who was always moving.

Anita had pulled him from rehab and given him a purpose. He had been on a downhill spiral. Drugs had become his life. There was nothing left but the clothes on his back.

He preferred speed. It was his drug of choice. He liked the way it made him feel.

Once a successful investment broker, he had worked long hours, and stalked women into the night. He had done that, as long as he could remember.

George was partial to prostitutes. They wouldn't be missed. Most of their families had forgotten about them anyway, they were throw aways.

He trolled the truck stops, for hookers. There was always one available. Lot lizards, as the truckers referred to them.

They loved his jacked up Chevy. He looked like he had money. It attracted them quicker than fly's to honey. All he had to do was sit there and rev up the truck a few times to get their attention. Before long there would be a knock on the window. George would smile, and say hello. Tell a story of how his wife didn't satisfy him and boom, they would climb right into the cab of his truck.

He would take them to the woods, and fuck them, real good the way those whores deserved. Then, in a flash he would plunge his knife into their abdomens and gut them. On some occasions he strangled them. It depended on what type of mood he was in.

Sometimes he buried them, sometimes not. He liked the thought of the animals, finishing off the rest, picturing them picking the flesh off the bones. He liked the feeling of their necks in his bare hands. It gave him power.

He kept their I.D.'s in a little box in the crawlspace of his house. A collector of sorts. Anita had watched him for a few weeks. She knew what he was. The day she had first spotted him, she knew.

One night, and a few speed balls too many, he had ended up in jail for driving his truck through the drive through window, of a McDonalds. He had been so fucked-up, he didn't even know where he was. The judge sentenced him to rehab.

The Pines Rehab Facility, at Lake Fester. That's where he officially met Anita.

Checking herself in was easy. Cash was all she needed. Anita confessed that she took too much speed, which ensured her place in the same program with George.

It seemed a lot of work to go through, but she was looking for a very specific person, a killer. Someone with no conscience.

Anita had befriended him, and after a few weeks she confessed to him why she was there, and that she appreciated what he was, and offered him a job. She had explained that his services would be needed, and his lifestyle would be accepted.

He took the offer willingly, and they checked out of rehab together.

 Now that she Anita had big plans for him, and Megan. Now that she had the child, she didn't need her daughter anymore. She was worthless to the cult now that she had reproduced.

 It was all revenge now. Anita wanted her dead. Sometimes she wanted to kill her herself, and she fantasized about it. Lying in her bed late at night, she thought up ways to kill her.

Other times, she thought she would just let George do it. A reprisal for all the trouble she had caused her. Maybe she would kill the other child first, a worthless boy. That would teach them. Show no mercy at all.

Then maybe kill Mark Westbrook slowly, Megan last, Make her suffer. Anita hated Megan so much, that it almost drove her mad.

She alone was responsible for the cult being disbanded, and for all the arrests and publicity. If the disc hadn't gotten to the press they would be home free.

It took her over a year, to relocate the headquarters to Texas, and Anita and her followers were working hard on increasing the numbers.

These things took time. She liked to mold her inner circle, pick only the chosen few. Francis, as he was now called, and George.

She needed him to control things that she could not. He was so grateful that she had brought him in that he would never turn against her. He was one of the faithful that deserved to sit in her inner circle.

George liked the fact that Anita worshiped him, and appreciated his skills. Here he didn't have to hide who he was. He was free to express his wants and needs as he pleased.

He didn't put much stock in her Bible, as she called it, but he carried a copy, and bowed his head at the ceremonies like a loyal follower.

Raven, as she called herself on stage, sat in front of the long mirror. The other girls were chatting among themselves.

Some were putting on makeup, others eating a quick meal that Callie, the house mom had cooked.

She was a busty blond who hailed from California.

Her unusually blue eyes had much too dark eye shadow, bright blue and dark red lipstick. Her hair was pinned up in a messy bun.

When her career as a stripper was over, she had taken over as the house mom.

The girls needed her. Strippers were notoriously unorganized. She provided all the things they needed. During the night there were usually two broken heels, and torn hose.

Callie made good living selling her meals and jewelry, stockings. The girls always forgot something, and it was all required wearing. No one went on stage unless their garb was complete.

She sold heels, and her items were pricy.

Makeup and bags and g strings were scattered on the white counter.

It was a usual night, and the activities were just getting started. It wasn't unusual for 20 or thirty girls to be in the club on any given night.

Raven took one last look. Her long dark hair that she had curled earlier was in a bun with long wisps of hair hanging, and framing her face.

Raven had a porcelain look to her, with high cheekbones and full red lips. She put on her red lipstick, and once she was satisfied with her results, she placed two small heart covered band aids over her nipples. It was required. She was glad for it. Raven didn't like being naked. Even if it was only from the waist up. It made her feel too vulnerable.

Anything to do with men made her feel that way, so she lost herself in the music, danced and forgot her troubles.

Although she had been stripping for a year, she still felt awkward, like she didn't quite belong. It wasn't who she was, only a means to an end. Pour some sugar on me resonated out of the speakers, as she glided around the pole gracefully.

Only recently had she started wearing a thong. Before it had been baby dolls, and negligées. Raven knew the ins and outs, but she never quite felt like herself.

In reality she wasn't herself anyway.

Some men had a way of making her feel cheap, although she stripped and did private dances, that was all. She wanted no part of the extracurricular activity, and the lifestyle that accompanied it. Some girls pulled in three to four thousand dollars a week, but they did anything and everything.

Raven worked two nights a week, and generally made a thousand, to twelve hundred. She was a hot commodity, and her looks made up for the extra activities that she wouldn't do. She was well respected by the owners, and the rest of the girls.

Raven was here to make money and to go home. She stayed out of the drama, and out of the drugs.

Two years ago, she had been thrown her into a downhill spiral. Life had been good before that, normal even. At 23 she had lived with her grandma, since birth, when her mother had died. They were close as two people could be and did everything together. Granny had nurtured and cared for her, always.

She was not Raven then, but Annie, as granny called her lovingly. Annie Moretti.

Isabella Moretti was of Italian descent, a small chubby woman with a grey bun. She had a thick Italian accent. Granny spent her days cooking and feeding everyone that would eat. The house always smelled of pasta and sauce. It was a warm homey feeling.

Her house looked like a typical grandma house. It was a small, white two bedroom cottage. A small picket graced the outside, and a stone walkway with little blue pansies ran parallel with the sidewalk.

There were light blue shutters on the windows. They didn't open but were decorative.

Inside there was the original hard wood floor. It was in good condition. Granny loved this floor and had it restored to its original beauty a few years prior. There were colorful throw rugs and the windows had colorful curtains.

The kitchen was tiny and cluttered with hundreds of spices, and many kitchen gadgets. This room opened into a small living room. The couch was draped with quilts and crochet blankets that granny had made over the years. It was home.

Annie attended the University of South Texas, and had just started as a freshman. She would move on into the clinical portion of the nursing program after her first year. Life was good. Stable, as it had always been.

On Tuesday she came home late from a class, and found Grannie on the floor. When the paramedics came it was too late. A massive stroke they had said.

Annie had begged them to do something, but they only shook their heads and apologized.

After the funeral Annie spent weeks mourning. She didn't go to school, much less leave the house. The bed was the most comfortable place. Every once in a while she got up and made a cup of coffee. Sometimes she ate a little something.

Annie had lost weight. Nothing was right anymore.

Her life seemed to be passing by her in a daze. It all seemed surreal. She tried to go back to school, but didn't quite fit in. There was a lot to take care of. No one had told her that there was so much to do when someone died.

People she knew from school called periodically, to check on her, and some just to be nosy.

When her friends finally coaxed her out, weeks later, she met Jim Burke. He was a short stocky young man, dark hair and even darker eyes, almost black. Not too bad looking, but not really her type. She was shy, and didn't have much experience with men. He came on strong, and was a braggart. Although he attended the same college, their paths had never crossed.

He was in Pre- med, and full of himself. He played Lacrosse, football Tennis and golf. He was muscular, but compact, and if you asked him he would tell you he was the greatest man that ever lived.

They went to a local club with friends. It made her feel a little better to be among people. It was the first time she had left the house since the funeral.

They laughed and danced. It felt good to be herself again. For the first time in weeks she felt happy. Annie thought maybe everything would be ok after all.

The rounds of drinks kept coming, and on the dance floor Jim had pulled her a little too close. His hands had a life of their own. She pushed his advances away several times, as he secretly got angrier and angrier.

When Annie returned from the bathroom, the pill he had slipped into her drink had had just enough time to dissolve. She sipped the drink, and when her friend asked her to dance she had guzzled the rest. That was her last memory.

She woke up 6 hours later bruised, naked, and alone in a hotel room. Annie thought of calling the police but was embarrassed and ashamed. The sheer thought of going through it, was just too much. Everything was too much. Dragging herself home somehow, she locked the doors behind herself and shut all the curtains.

Granny was dead and she was alone in the world. There was no one to help her, no one to turn to. Now she had been beaten and raped. Annie stood in the shower and sobbed. Her body had been scrubbed clean, in the hot streaming water, her skin pink, and stinging from the abuse.

It was unbearable. Her head ached, but that was nothing compared to her heart. It hurt like nothing else ever had.

She could no longer face this cruel world. Everything she loved had been taken from her, her family, her pride, and every ounce of self- respect, most importantly her peace of mind.

She didn't feel safe in the house she had grown up in. Shadows loomed around every corner. The fear of going out was overwhelming. This was no way to live.

Suddenly it was clear. Annie knew what she had to do. She tidied the house, and made her bed. She didn't want anyone thinking bad about her, and Granny.

It would be expected that the place was in order, as it had always been.

Once everything was done, she ate a bowl of her favorite ice cream. Savoring every bite.

An hour later, she was behind the wheel of Granny's car, heading out to the Sound. When the cliffs came into view, the tears were streaming down her face. She had lost everything. She closed her eyes as the vehicle went over the embankment.

The car had flipped over several times. She was ejected, and lay bleeding in the snow. Annie lay on her back on the icy ground, and looked up at the stars. At first the cold had been so heavy …….. now, as she slowly felt herself fading, a warm feeling came over her, and the pain was gone.

When she looked up she saw a bright light. It became larger and larger and formed a sort of hallway in front of her.

Annie stood and walked into the tunnel. She couldn't remember why, only that it was right. She walked along until the light- tunnel opened up into a field.

It was a meadow. The birds were chirping and singing. Wild flowers grew in abundance, along with meadows of sunflowers. The yellow and orange hues bright and glowing. She was warm and everything was right. She had no more sorrow or pain. She could feel the warmth of the sun on her shoulders.

Annie walked toward a wooden bench that stood in the center of the field. A man rested there, quiet and still. She sat, and turned to the man sitting beside her. It was the most natural thing to do.

He was older, much older, with piercing blue eyes and a long white beard.

He spoke to her, but not with words. His lips never moved, yet she could hear him clearly. His voice deep and clear.

"Annie, it's not time for you yet. I have something that I need you to do first."

He placed his warm hand on hers. Annie felt a surge go through her.

It was like ten thousand volts of electricity. It was not painful, just powerful.

"You are very important. Go now. Go back....."

Suddenly she was laying back in the snow, with the paramedics bending over her.

"We got her back," she heard the one say.

Annie felt herself being loaded into the ambulance.

The lights of the world seemed to fly by her. She could hear the sirens, and every few minutes a face came into view. It was a nice face, full of kindness. The first face she had seen when she had returned.

"Stay with me Annie," the paramedic said.

He held her hand, and talked her through. They hadn't expected any survivors when they reached the scene. The twisted metal, mixed with blood and snow, presented a gruesome scene.

After several days in the hospital, it was determined that she had no major injuries.

According to the doctor's it was a miracle. People came from all over the hospital to see the miracle girl found below the embankment.

On Monday the transport service picked her up, and she went home to Granny's house, alone. The silence was deafening. She slept, and dreamed about the field, and the old man.

Annie could still hear the voice in her head. It was hard to tell if it was genuine, or if it had been just a dream after all.

His hand had felt so real. It was warm, his skin paper thin. He must have been an angel, or the big man himself. Maybe she was going crazy. That was a definite possibility.

She had told no one. Who would believe it anyway. Before the accident she felt like giving up. Now, something in her, told her to hang on, that there was more to it. She would just have to wait, till it came to her. For now an unseen force seemed to guide her along, and that was enough.

Her depression was gone. She didn't know why. Annie had never been a religious person. There was no talk of God growing up. Granny had avoided the subject when it presented itself. She was forbidden to attend church with friends when she was small. There were invitations to Sunday school, and picnics, but the answer was always no.

They had never talked about it. Once she had asked Grandpa why they didn't attend the church that her friends and neighbors attended.

Gramps had simply said, "It's just not for us."

Annie never remembered attending any church.

"Why isn't it for us?" she had pushed.

"Because I said so." He had growled.

That had to be explanation enough, because what Gramps said, is what it was. It was the law of the house. Granny didn't even go against him. No one did. He was not a friendly man. He provided for his family financially, but that was all. In him there was no love lost for anyone.

When she was thirteen Ms. Schwartz her English teacher gave her a small bible. Annie kept it hidden under her mattress. She had read it from top to bottom. It was well worn.

Annie knew that her living through this accident had been nothing short of a miracle. When they asked her, she had lied, and told them she fell asleep at the wheel. No one questioned her bruises. They just assumed that they were from the wreck. Even the bruises on her inner thighs never came up.

To the paramedics and police it was cut and dry. The investigation was closed.

Although the bills were piling up, all her hopelessness was gone. Somehow she felt a purpose, a drive. Her body was healing, the bruises fading. Her pride had not really returned, but knowing she had to keep the house, Annie dropped out of college, and looked for a job.

There was a small life insurance policy that had been left to her.

It paid for the funeral and the few left over bills, but now most of the money was gone. In a few weeks there would be none at all.

Annie answered an ad for "Kittens" It was a high class strip club. The manager told her to come in and audition. As she stepped into the building, her eyes adjusted to the light. It was dusky, the walls dark red velvet, and soft lights shone on them. To the left there was a long bar with mirrors. Several stages and cages were scattered around the room. At any given time there were at least 20 dancers on the floor. Music blared from every corner, a slow song, Poison, she thought.

To the side were the isolated rooms, for lap dances, and private sittings with the higher paying clientele. When she walked up on the stage, the manager had asked her name... it was then, at that moment, that Raven was born.

Mark had driven all day. They had spent the night in hazard, and had gotten back on the road early that morning.

After almost a year and a half, there was finally a solid lead. Something they could sink their teeth into.

Mark had been glad for it. He knew if they sat waiting much longer Megan would have gone absolutely crazy. The only thing keeping her sane was Sam. He grew like a weed, and was never quiet. He babbled to anyone that would listen, and to himself. He was active and you couldn't take your eyes off of him for a second.

They had been waiting, checking out every lead. It had been like pissing in the wind. Nothing had panned out. Mark knew it was a waiting game. They had to be patient till Anita resurfaced, and that wouldn't happen till the heat died down, and until she felt safe enough to reorganized her following.

Once they left the hospital, they had moved into the compound with Grey. It was the safest place for them. It was the one place they could defend, if need be.

Sam loved the horses, and Megan cherished the seclusion, and the comfort it provided, in this dark time.

When the call came in, they were on the road in less than an hour. They had all know this day would come.

Tom sat in the seat beside Mark. Megan was in the back of the Jeep with Sam. At two and a half, he was unusually tall for his age, with blond curly hair, and sky blue eyes.

They were headed west, to New Mexico. Tom had gotten word that the cult was re-organizing in Texas. Although they had known it from the start that she had a stronghold there, Texas was a big place and it was like a needle in a haystack.

Now there was solid information, something to go on. Mark and Grey wanted to be closer, so they could take trips over the border and search for the child. That, would come first, before anything else.

Megan had been quiet the last few weeks. She was a good mother and cared for Sammy as she lovingly called him. It was short for Samuel Jack Westbrook.

Grey lovingly referred to him as the little hippie, due to his long blond curls.

He had grown attached to him over the last few years. The little boy lit up the house, and his spirits, like nothing else had in many years. He had felt no joy since his daughter and wife had died, until now. He knew that they still had a lot of ground to cover, but the little guy just melted his heart.

It would probably take a few more months to get enough Intel, to have a solid idea of where they may be, but at least they had finally resurfaced. Everyone was glad, to finally be doing something.

The waiting had been the worst.

Grey had watched Mark and Megan slowly sink further and further down, into their own hell. They had grown apart, shutting each other out. It was evident to everyone but them. They didn't really argue, but they were becoming like shadows, passing each other in the hall, barely uttering a word.

Although they were good parents, Grey could see it spiraling down. He knew it had affected their relationship, and it crossed his mind, that it may be worse torture not to know what happened to your child, but then other times he thought that for them, at least there was always hope.

Megan's hope never faltered.

Mark on the other hand was a realist, and he had seen too much death in his life. He was all about the odds, and when he tried to discuss it with Megan, she became angry and distant. It was something they would never agree on.

He was trying to help her cope, in case the worst happened, but she refused to let him alter her hope. It was all that kept her going.

There had been several murders across New Mexico, and Tom thought it was somehow related. Grey followed them in a large black f-350.

He was on edge. At the compound he felt like the child was safe. He could make sure no harm came his way. Here in the open there was too much risk. There was nowhere to leave them though.

No place was safe. Megan would have never stayed behind anyway.

He was prepared to kill everyone and everything, to save Sam and his sister. He remembered what it felt like to have a family and to lose them. He would do anything he could do to make sure that never happened again. He sure didn't want to see anyone else go through the same thing.

Mark drove on, lost in his thoughts. He was not the same. The joy he had felt when he found Megan and his son had been short lived.

Grey had seen the color drain out of his face when he had learned of the second baby. It started a new nightmare, far worse than the first.

He spent the last two years sinking further and further into his guilt. He had lost weight, and it showed on his face. Now he at least had some hope that they would find their baby. One way or another, he would bring her home. Dead or alive. The thought of that turned something inside of him. He couldn't quite put his finger on it, but Mark knew it had changed him.

Megan had refused to name their daughter. She said she would name her when she was back in her arms. Hope was the one thing she had left.

Most nights she cried herself to sleep. It broke his heart. He hoped the she was still alive, but he knew the odds, but since Tom had recently acquired a bible from the children of the rainbow, they knew the ceremony could not take place until after the solstice, following the child's third birthday. There was some hope, but time was running out.

Mark felt detached, unable to picture anything about her. Grey said it was because he had not seen her, and she didn't seem real to him. He supposed this was true. It made sense.

It had been weeks, with no lead, and although he tried to remain positive for Megan's sake he was a realist and his hope was beginning to fade.

The only hope he had left, was another crazy ritual, and he hoped there was still time. Anita had disappeared into the wind like a ghost, for all this time.

It was no way to live. Megan had Sam. He felt like an outsider looking in. He loved her and his son, but the detached feeling would not leave him.

Tom reminded him daily that there was hope. He didn't care. Tom's words meant nothing to him. The only person that even remotely knew what he was going through was Grey.

He thought back to all the years they had served together. They had been through some shit. Maybe this was some sort of punishment for the things they had done for their country. "In the name of freedom."

What a fucking joke that had been. The government was more corrupt, than any third world country. They had both learned that, the hard way. Mark had seen it first hand when they left him to rot, in a third world shit hole. He realized quickly that they weren't coming back for him. He was not going to be their fall guy. He got out and hiked cross country to Malaisia, where he holed up drunk till Grey came to retrieve him.

Grey had gotten his education the day his family died. The safe house had been compromised by an inside leak. A mole. The Cia had done nothing to help him, except let him go. They cut their losses and ran. Hell he didn't blame them for that. They alone, had turned him into three-hundred pounds of hate.

He had trained most of them, and they knew what he was capable of.

He had been there. Something didn't feel right. Grey had driven down the road on sheer instinct, in the direction the car had taken. When they arrived, the car was pulled to the side of the road. The door stood open. The driver and the guards, gone. Mark saw it first. Molly lay in the snow, holding her baby girl. Both throats had been cut.

Mark remembered how her red hair had blended with the blood and snow. It was surreal. He had tried to head him off, but there was no stopping him. Grey had come around the car and for a moment, he stood, silent and still, starring at the scene in front of him. Then he hit his knees, cradling his wife and child.

He screamed……. a deep guttural scream. Then there was only silence, as he rocked them. Mark remembered the snow, you could hear it falling. It was eerie.

He had called for reinforcement. Grey rode with the bodies. He refused to leave them. No one had the balls to try to stop him anyway.

There was no budging him. He left when he was ready. He walked out of the hospital, heading for the office. Mark followed him, knowing what was about to happen. Grey refused to speak. He thought about calling ahead, to warn them, but then thought better of it.

They had it coming.

Grey threw open the door, shattering the glass. It didn't phase him. He walked straight up to the Hank, the driver of the car, that had picked up his family.

"We changed cars." He cried, but it made no difference. Grey had slammed his head into the desk ten or twelve times, by the time they managed to pull him off.

Even with six men holding him back, he managed to tear up the rest of the place, and anyone that got in his way.

Finally, when he heard the sirens, he stood still, as if he was listening to something that only he could hear.

His nine in his hand.

Mark wasn't sure what was happening, but he managed to make eye contact, and Grey allowed himself to be dragged out of the door.

The funeral was no better. The Cia had attempted to pay, and Mark didn't even like to think about what Grey had done with the check, before sending it back.

Toilet paper was the politest analogy.

They had put their money together, and three days later, they were shoulder to shoulder, in front of the caskets.

Grey never shed a tear. Mark could see him shaking as he stood with him, to say goodbye. When they lowered the caskets into the ground, it was all he could take.

He walked away, and locked himself in his fortress, refusing to see anyone, except Mark. He had stayed for a year, and finally went on his way. Mark needed to work. He was no good sitting idle.

He would never leave a man behind, and neither would Grey. They understood each other, and no matter what happened they would always be brothers, maybe not by blood, but by sweat, grime, heartbreak and loyalty.

The silence was shattered when Grey's voice boomed over the CB.

"Hey, when are we stopping? You planning on driving straight through?"

"Yes. It's not that much further." Mark said quietly.

"Well your wife and MY baby need to stretch pretty soon."

Tom shook his head and smiled. He was so inappropriate.

"Fine, I'll find a restaurant. We'll stop and get something to eat."

"Thank god I'm wilting away to nothing." Grey groaned.

 At 260 pounds he was hardly wilting, but he had made it his mission to annoy Mark as often as possible to keep him out of his rut, he was slowly sliding into. Grey understood it better that anyone could.

Mark pulled the truck off the highway. They had just entered Bernalillo County. It was on the outskirts of Albuquerque. He really had no plans, on where they would stay. He thought this place was as good as any. It didn't matter to him. He was tired.

All he needed was a quiet place to lay his head. He didn't give a fuck about the scenery. Mark had lost something. He was down and felt like he was responsible for the baby being gone. He couldn't shake it.

Steering the truck into the Santa Fe Inn, he decided it looked like a good place to stay. Megan would like it. He tried his best to always do things that would please her. Not to keep the peace, like some men, but because he genuinely loved her.

Plus it had a restaurant, and it would get Grey off his back. He acted like he would die if he didn't get a meal every few hours. It had always been this way but it drove everyone crazy.

Mark helped Megan with Sam, while the men grabbed the luggage.

"How many suitcases can one small Kid have?" Grey complained.

"They are the bags of both children," Megan said softly. "I'm going to need supplies when we find her." He starred at her. He should have known.

"I got the dumb ass on me." Grey stated, hanging his head. He generally said the wrong things, around women. "It's ok." She smiled at him and patted him on his shoulder.

She always had a way of making him feel better when he knew he was acting stupid. He loved her, like he loved Mark and the kids. They had become his family.

Megan awed when they entered the lobby. It was large, all made of clay. Shadows danced on the clay walls, and gave the entire room a warm glow.

The ceilings were high and there were chandeliers with candles everywhere. It gave the room a mystic sort of warmth, around the floor and perimeter of the room were bowls, with candles flickering. It was not unusual for this area, but Megan had never seen anything so inviting, and magical.

They rented two rooms, and dropped off their luggage. Mark and Tom had gotten a table already. Grey waited for Megan.

Tom pulled out a map of the area, both of them leaned over studying it intently. They raised their heads and looked at each other when the ruckus started. Mark jumped up first and headed for the lobby.

"No Indians in here. You have to go or I will call the sheriff."

Megan saw the old grey haired Apache woman, as they entered the lobby. Her braids hung down both sides of the shawl that covered her. She was old, but had bright blue eyes.

Their eyes met and she walked straight to Megan and Sam. Grey stepped in front of her, his weapon drawn.

Megan pushed him aside lightly. "It's ok," giving him a scowling look. "Calm down."

Somehow she knew this woman meant her no harm. Seraphine took Megan's hand in hers. She had long seen the future but had not had a vision as clear as this, in many years.

"You have lost something......the white giant, and the dark lady, have stolen from you. They mean you much harm. I see her.....baby Josephine. She is waiting for you. She is very important. The Raven will guide you to her."

Megan starred at her, as the old woman suddenly let go of her hand.

Her breath caught in her throat. Tears came to her eyes immediately.

The pain had been so unbearable for her. No one could understand the feeling of despair that she had been going through. It was hers alone. Like a hole in her heart that could never fill completely.

"Where is she?" she sobbed. "Can you tell me?" Grey placed a protective hand on her shoulder.

"I do not know, but this causes you much pain. I know this much." She said gently.

Mark and Tom had walked up to see what was going on. Grey held up his hand to silence them.

The old woman took her hand once again.

"There is a mountain surrounded by sand. I see a stone wall with drawings, It is a cold place. There are many enemies. The Raven will be your salvation."

"What is the Raven?" Megan asked.

"She is dark, but light. You will come to know her in time." She bent down to Sam, and took his small hand in hers.

"You will do much good in the world, little man."

"That's enough," Grey said, pushing her away from the child. "Don't touch him."

Seraphine smiled at him, and gave him a knowing look. It made him very uncomfortable.

"I must go." She squeezed Megan's hand, and turned to Mark. "When you get where you are going, you must find Kona. He will help you." She turned and walked out of the door.

Megan looked at the three men starring at her. Tears in her eyes, but for once they were happy ones.

"My baby girl is alive, and her name is Josephine."

Mark and Tom exchanged knowing glances.

Megan walked into the restaurant.

"What the hell was that?" he whispered to Grey, pulling him aside.

"She was some kind of fortune teller."

"I don't want some freak show filling Megan's head full of bullshit and false hope. You know better than that. You should have shut that shit down."

Grey starred at him. He was also a realist, and he didn't really understand the full jest of what had just happened, but it had renewed his hope. Grey didn't know why, but he believed her.

"Let her have hope. It's all we've got right now." Grey said giving his shoulder a squeeze.

"Bullshit." Mark replied, slapping it away, and heading to the table.

For the first time in weeks Megan ate a complete meal. While they ate, Grey repeated what Seraphine had said.

Tom and Mark exchanged glances. Megan stopped eating and laid down her fork. She looked at them both.

"You don't believe it, do you?" she said quietly.

"I believe it." The deep voice said quietly, as Grey looked her in the eyes.

"Come on Man," Tom said. "Be serious, there is no way that crazy woman knows anything." He looked over at Mark for support. Mark looked up, just in time to have all eyes on him.

"I don't know... I believe in facts, and numbers, things I can put my hands on."

He reached over and touched Megan's hand. "I don't want you to get your hopes up and be pulled into some crazy lady's rant."

She pulled her hand away, shaking her head. "You didn't hear everything she said, or see her face. She said the White giant and the dark lady have stolen from you. She knew about OUR daughter, and that she was stolen. How would she know that?"

Her voice was harsh now. It pissed her off that he didn't believe her. She slammed her knife down on the table.

"Babe, I just don't see how it's possible that's all I'm saying. It's a coincidence. People like that know how to play on your emotions. You hear about it all the time. They say things and desperate people hear what they want."

Grey starred at him. He knew it was about to go down.

She glared at him. "Grey believes me."

Now Grey could feel them all starring, at him.

He averted his eyes. No matter what he said now he would be in trouble, so he just kept quiet. They finished their meal in silence, only Tom and Grey making polite small talk.

Afterwards everyone headed to their room, Mark following Megan in silence.

She put the sleeping child down on the bed and changed his clothes and diaper without him waking up. He was a quiet, good little boy. He slept like a rock.

Gently, she put him in the middle of the second bed and placed pillows all around him, to keep him from rolling off. She was too tired to set up the portable crib tonight.

He was almost three, and was slow to walk. He had just started to pull himself up on things. What he lacked in walking, he made up with babbling. He talked like crazy, all day long. It seemed no one but Grey understood him. She wasn't really sure if he even did, or if he just guessed.

She smiled at the thought. They were a funny pair. The iron giant and the blond hippie child.

Mark came out of the shower a few minutes later. Megan sat on the bed and looked at him. The tension cut the air like a knife.

"Look, he said softly, I don't want you be upset with me. I don't want anyone to hurt you. I don't know what's going on right now. I want to believe it, just as much as you, but this isn't my sort of thing. I know facts. I'm black and white."

He touched her hand again, hoping she wouldn't pull away.

"Facts are not always all there is. It's not all cut and dry."

"I just don't want you to have false hope."

"False hope? So you think our daughter is dead."

"No..."

"Then how can we not have any hope? That's all I have. It's the only thing that gets me through the day." He tears flowed now.

He hated it when she cried. He pulled her into his arms. It had been a year and a half of hell. "Don't cry." He stroked her back, holding her tightly.

"I have to take a shower." She pulled away from him and shut the bathroom door behind herself. Mark ran his hand through his hair. It was so hard for him to believe. He only knew what he could touch and feel. The whole thing sounded crazy to him.

He didn't want her to have a big let -down. He had read about these psychics, sometimes they just hit it lucky.

He heard the water running. Crossing the room he pulled the door open and saw her through the shower door. He dropped his pants and followed her in. Mark stepped into the shower. The steam filled the walk in shower. He reached for her, and pulled her close to him. Kissing her neck and shoulders. "I'm sorry." he murmured.

"I just don't want anyone hurting you." Megan turned and looked into his eyes. She knew he meant it. She touched his cheek gently, as he leaned down and kissed her. He pulled her up into his arms against the shower wall. He made love to her as the hot steamy water beat down on their skin.

The next morning Mark packed the truck in silence. Megan and Grey made small talk over breakfast. Tom was sleeping in. He wasn't much of a morning person.

Grey held the Sam, as they checked out of the hotel. He could see the tension on their faces. It had been hard on them both, and Mark could be a hard ass when it came to showing his feelings.

Not so good. One thing Death had taught Grey was never to take people for granted. He starred at Mark.

Mark met his eyes, as Grey raised one eyebrow at him.

"What?" he said defensively, throwing his hands up.

Grey shook his head and sighed.

"You're a stupid Motherfucker." Grey announced.

"Yeah? How so?" Mark was up in his face in an instant.

"You have a chance to be part of something here and your acting dumb as hell."

"I'm sure you're much better qualified to handle my wife." Grey starred at him.

"What did you say?" Now he was getting pissed off.

"I'm not repeating it."

"Because you know its bullshit. I'm helping her. Someone has to. You're so damn caught up in your own shit that you can't see what's right in front of your face. Now back out of my face before I lay you out."

Tom walked up. "Hey guys? What's going on?" he said lightly, knowing they were about to throw down.

"Nothing." Mark grumbled as he turned and walked away.

They drove all day in silence. Even Sam slept. Megan starred out the window watching the scenery go by. She was thinking of her daughter wondering if she had the same blond curly hair that Sam had. She had pictured her, in her mind a thousand times.

She felt a relief, and a sadness, thinking of what Seraphine had said. She did believe her, but she was afraid to let her guard down.

Towards nightfall they entered the small town of pueblo. It was west of all the big towns, and bordered the desert and beyond that, the Superstition Mountains.

It gave Megan a chill when she saw the mountains bordering on the sand, just as Seraphine had predicted.

There were a few buildings in town and a small grocery store. Grey and Megan purchased supplies, and it was near dark when they reached the large cabin. It had cooled down significantly, and Megan shivered.

The cabin was made completely of clay and could house 12 people. Inside the southwestern style deco made it cozy and warm. It had served as a bunk house in its day, but now as some of the ranches had folded up, it served as a rental.

The dessert temperature dropped drastically at night, and everyone was glad to be inside. Mark walked the inside of the cabin, while Grey checked the perimeter.

Once he was sure it was safe, the men unloaded the truck, while Megan took Sam inside. As they brought in the last load Grey slapped Mark on the butt.

"Hey sweetness....you gonna make me dinner?"

Mark shook his head and smiled. He couldn't stand him sometimes, but he knew he was wrong.

"Your fat enough. You can live off the land." He teased.

Megan smiled at Grey having to duck in all the doorways. "These damn Indians must be short as hell." He grumbled. "I'm starving."

He made her laugh. He was either complaining about starving to death, which was impossible with his mountainous frame, or he was bumping into things and griping about short people.

She hoped someday he would find someone to love. Someone that would appreciate his Quirky sense of humor, and that could stand up to him, when he threw a fit.

Megan claimed the middle bedroom, with no windows. She felt safer that way. Mark lay down across the bed. He was tired from driving, and his back and neck hurt like hell. Sam was already asleep in his playpen.

"Grey sent Tom to town for dinner, before he dies." They both laughed.

"You ok?" Megan asked.

"Yeah babe, I'm just worn out." He smiled at her catching her hand in his, as she walked by.

"Are you ok?"

"Yes." She smiled, a tired smile. Exhaustion had settled in. Between taking care of Sam, and the never ending traveling, she was just done. Longing for a home, her home. The ranch. Missing the Florida sun, and the ocean, and the way things used to be.

 She wished her father could be here with her, Mark, and both her children. In a perfect world. That would be wonderful.

"Megan?"

"What?" suddenly she was back in reality.

"What are you thinking about?"

"I was thinking about home and Dad, and how nice it would be to have a normal life." She squeezed his hand.

"I know. I wish that for us too. I know I don't always say it, but I want those things." He pulled her down next to him.

"I love you. I do, and I don't want this to come between us. We have to stick together. I know I'm an ass, and I don't always say the right things." He kissed her lips, hugging her to him. She held onto him, and pressed her face into his chest. His scent made her feel safe. They had been through so much together, almost loosing each other forever.

"I know you mean well." She said kissing him again.

"I do." He murmured, unbuttoning her blouse. When they had the chance to be close to each other, they grabbed on to any moment they could find. No matter what was between them. They had held on to each other for comfort for the last year and a half, and the more time went by the harder it was.

They both knew time was running out, but at this moment all that mattered was their love for each other.

The club was crowded on Friday night. The music blared, and the crowd was in rare form. Between the football players and the regulars, it was packed to the gills.

The entire team was in town for the playoffs. They loved the club, and dropped an obscene Amount of money. The girls worked double shifts to appease all the players.

Raven was in rare form, dancing to all her favorite songs. They loved her. She was a crowd favorite by far one of the best looking girls in the club. They demanded an encore twice, and by 5 am her feet ached and she was tired and hungry.

The floor guy swept the bills off the stage and brought them to her, in a paper bag. It was a good shift for her. She had cleared over two grand tonight.

After tipping everyone out, she dressed into her street clothes, Tucking Granny's necklace into her shirt.

She had worn it since Granny had died, never taking it off.

"What are you going to do tonight?" Lupe asked. She was American Indian and a beautiful girl. She lived just over the border, with her Grandmother. Supporting herself, and helping with the household bills.

Lupe had long dark hair, and dark eyes, she braided her hair and wore a handmade beaded buckskin dress with matching moccasins. Her large breasts filled it out perfectly. The out of towners loved it. She loved to dance to Indian outlaw. The Football players got a kick out of it, and thought she was a real life wild squaw.

"I don't know do you want to get something to eat?" Raven said.

"I'm starving." She stuffed her remaining things in her stripper bag as she fondly called it. "If I don't get food I'm gonna die."

"Me too." Lupe laughed. "Let's go to the waterhole. It's got food all night."

"Dude, that's way over the border. I don't want to be out all night." Raven complained.

"We won't be," Lupe replied. She knew Raven whined when she was hungry. "We can eat and you can spend the night at my house."

Raven sighed. She just wanted to get in her own bed, but the food was too tempting to say no too. She was starving.

Lupe packed her things into her red duffle bag. She had changed into jeans a white t- shirt and sneakers.

She was a good girl. Once she had, had a boyfriend in town, but it didn't last. She had grown up with the old people and was a serious person.

Her mother had died an alcoholic; her father had shot himself, the same night. Grandmother had taken her in, and raised her. The two girls had a lot in common. It formed a strange bond that drew them together.

The bouncer walked them to Ravens car.

The club took the security of the girls serious. Three strippers had disappeared in the last 6 months. No one had heard from them again. Joslin and Sandi had no family to speak of, but when Carrie had disappeared the FBI had gotten involved.

Her sister was a hot shot lawyer in El Paso, and an Indian to boot, whose extended family still lived on the reservation. Once the media had gotten ahold of the story it took off like wildfire.

The police had been all over the club. Now the Tribal council was also involved. It affected their own. It was the business of the tribe, not the FBI, yet they cooperated, to an extent.

The tribal council was upset that the first two girls didn't get any attention. They had no one looking for them, and were considered disposable by some.

Business at the club had suffered a little with all the police presence, but Raven had saved up a nice nest egg. She would be fine.

As usual against everyone's advice Lupe had hitched a ride there, and would be riding back with Raven.

They locked the doors, as the bouncer walked away.

"You should stop hitch hiking." Raven said.

"Girl I've lived here my whole life. I'm careful. Nothing is going to happen to me. I'm an Indian outlaw." She joked.

They had, had this conversation a hundred times. It was futile. No matter what Raven said, Lupe did what she wanted. She had lived here since she was born. She knew it would never happen to her. Besides she was still saving for a car, and until she got one, she had to do, what she had to do.

The FBI continued to make their presence known, but life at the club went back to normal. The media had found new stories to report on, and people stopped paying attention.

The two girls were laughing and joking, as they pulled out of the parking lot, neither of them noticing the black cargo van easing in behind them.

George licked his lips. It had been too long, a whole month since the last girl.

He took his time choosing them. Only a specific type was on his radar. Only the perfect ones. To him it was an art. He was very selective.

Parking across the street from the small restaurant, he waited, and watched.

Through the window, he could see the girls eating and laughing.

George had watched Lupe for two weeks. He had almost snagged her earlier in the day, as she hitch hiked, but then at the last second, a car had picked her up. He had met her at the club, a few weeks ago, and she had danced just for him. Then he saw her dance for another man. It was unforgivable. She was a tease.

He had punched the ceiling of the van till his knuckles bled. That was ok though. It only made the hunt sweeter. He would put her in her place, then she would be forgiven, and be perfect forever.

Now here, he had his chance again. He was a little concerned that there were two of them, but he would kill the tall girl, and then have his fun with Lupe.

He liked to keep them for a while. Take his time.

He saw them get up, and walk to the checkout. George perked up. This was it.

Once he started the van, he pulled along the side of Ravens car. The girls came out still chatting and giggling. Before they knew was happening George had grabbed Raven by the hair, his knife out in a flash.

He had planned every detail. He would slit her throat and she would bleed out quickly.

Then he would run the other one down.....the hunt was the best part, it made him feel like a god.

He loved to hear their rasping breath as he chased them. It gave him a high almost as good as the moment he ended their lives.

Raven saw the knife flash, "RUN!" she screamed. The blade stopped suddenly.

Lupe ran. George starred down at her, still holding the knife to her throat.

He grabbed her necklace.

"Where did you get this?" He spat, starring down at the pendant, as he loosened his grip on her hair.

"TELL ME" he demanded.

"Fuck off you creep" She screamed in his face, clawing at him.

He dragged her into the van. They struggled as he held the chloroform covered cloth over her mouth. By the time she stopped fighting George was sweating.

He didn't know what the fuck was going on. The necklace had stopped him dead in his tracks. He knew anyone wearing the Serpents pendant was protected.

He slammed the van door shut.

"FUCK" he cursed, slapping himself in the head.

When he calmed himself down, he climbed back into the van and tied Ravens hands and feet. George then searched the highway for Lupe. He was pissed.

A distraction had cost him his mark. Odds of finding her now were slim.

He punched the ceiling again and cursed his bleeding knuckles. He wanted to kill her. His rage was insatiable. He starred at the limp body in the back. She was of no use to him.

She was not the chosen one, but he could not kill her. The necklace gave her protection. It was absolutely forbidden.

George was a monster. Nothing much scared him. There was only one thing in the world he was afraid of…. Anita. He would not go against her, or the cult. He had seen what they were capable of, watching their sick ceremonies, had given him all the insight he needed.

Lupe ran like she had never run before, tears flowing down her face. She sobbed uncontrollably, and moved quickly through the darkness.

She should have stayed and helped Raven. When she heard her scream run, her legs seemed to have a life of their own.

Lupe ran across the road, into the corn field. She had to stay off the highway.

She moved between the rows, the corn was tall, and the stalks were narrow.

Once deep in the corn, she crawled on her hands and knees and then stopped, listening for the man, doing her best to control her breathing.

Lupe pictured her spirit animal, and took a few deep breaths to calm herself.

She had to be quiet and go for help, if nothing else to survive, and to save Raven.

All she could hear was her own heartbeat. It was pounding in her throat. She was afraid he would hear it and find her.

Lupe held her hands over her mouth to stifle the sobs that came again. Crouching down, she slowed her breathing once again and listened. The only audible sound was the crickets. They chirped loudly, filling the night, with their high pitched screeches.

Once again, Lupe started to crawl slowly through the columns of corn.

The smell of the fields filled her nostrils, and she could feel the dirt gathering under her fingernails. Her knees stung, and she was sure they were bleeding.

Periodically she could feel a small rock digging into her skin, as she crawled along.

Finally after what seemed like hours, a small clearing came into view. She could hear a vehicle on the highway. Instinctively she knew it was the van searching for her.

She eased back into the concealment of the corn. Sitting here, crouched down ready to run, but forcing herself to wait, till the sun came up.

There were no cars in sight, yet she could still hear the engine of the van patrolling around the nearby streets. He didn't give up easily. He was pissed.

Someone was going to pay.

Lupe ran across the fields. He shoes had been lost, and her feet were also bleeding. She knew the area, and stayed off the highway.

When the house came into sight...tears sprang from her eyes, and sobs escaped her throat. This house was her home, her safety. Once she reached the entryway she pounded on the door with both hands, screaming.

"HELP ME." Her small fists pounding harder.

The door opened and she collapsed into her Grandmothers arms. Seraphine led her to the small table, and although she knew from her vision, that the dark man had come, she let Lupe tell her the story.

Seraphine brewed her a cup of tea and a few minutes later when her uncle Redbird, the leader of the tribal council and the town sheriff came, he drove her to the police station.

Lupe gave her statement, and was asked to wait for a man from the FBI. Tom was the first to receive the call. He slowly hung up the receiver and turned to the curious faces of his friends.

"There has been another attack. Two girls, except this time we have a witness."

He stated, as they followed him out to the truck.

Tom felt his heart beat quicken. He knew this was it, the break they had been waiting for.

"This may be a good lead for us. Do you want to come with me?"

Mark wanted to go, but he remembered the last time he had let his guard down.

He didn't want to leave Megan or Sam. Megan watched his face. She knew he blamed himself.

"Go, we will be fine. Please. You need this. Grey will babysit me."

She smiled and touched his face. "Go."

"That's right." Grey said, and winked at him sarcastically.

"I'm qualified."

"I can't stand you, you prick." He boldly told him.

Tom pulled the truck onto the highway.

They rode in silence each lost in their thoughts. The last time he had been in this truck Tom had taken him to the digs….. how he had dreaded each one, hoping to get some closure, but praying that he would not find Megan, or Grey, in the mounds of bodies.

He couldn't believe the wake of destruction that this group had left behind. It was unheard of. They had operated right under the nose of the police and the FBI.

Even now that he knew she was alive, the memory was still unbearable. He had fallen apart, convinced that his life was over.

He had almost ended it all. Now he had everything to live for. He had prayed that this would bring them one step closer to finding his daughter. No matter what anyone said he would always blame himself.

Every night when he hugged his son, he wondered about his daughter, if she was still alive, and what the coming days would bring. He fought with himself, knowing that if they didn't find her in time, she would be sacrificed.

It was the worst thing he could ever imagine. He prayed that if it came to that, he would not be alive to see it. Not that he was being a coward. He was nothing of the sort, but he knew how much he could take, and that was way over the line.

He didn't know if Megan could survive the loss of a child.

Seeing the love she had for Sam, he prayed that they would find a happy ending.

Before he knew it they had pulled up in front of a small clay building. Mark exited the truck and followed Tom inside.

A large man of American Indian descent came toward them.

"I am Redbird. I am what you call a sheriff in town, the tribal elder. The young woman you are about to question is my niece."

He ushered them into a small interrogation room.

"I will be in the room with you." It wasn't a question but a statement.

After what she had been through he wasn't about to leave her alone with these men. He had already checked their credentials, but still he trusted no one. He was a giant of a man, as tall as Grey.

He had dark reddish skin and a long braid on both sides with red and white beads intertwined. An eagle feather braided into the left side.

Lupe sat at the end of the table. She looked small and frail.

Her hair was a mess, and small pieces of corn husks and dirt were evident. Streaks were dried down her cheeks from many tears.

She sat with her hands folded in her lap. The men sat down. Tom guessed she was 18 at best. Just a child.

Redbird sat down next to her and touched her hand with his massive one.

"Lupe…" these men are here to speak with you. They are from the FBI. Can you tell them what you told me?"

Lupe looked at them both for a few moments. She told them of her friendship with Raven, and how the girls had left the club together.

"What happened when you walked outside?" did you notice anything unusual?" Tom asked.

"No… the bouncer walked us to the car. We were laughing and joking. We drove to the restaurant and ate.

When we came out he was waiting for us. I didn't see him till it was too late." Her voice began to shake. Tears now flowed down her cheeks.

He grabbed Raven and had a knife to her throat. I didn't know what to do…then she yelled for me to run. So I ran." She sobbed.

"Oh my god, I know he killed her. I left her, and ran away." She dropped her head into her hands and sobbed louder.

The room was quiet. Redbird met Marks eyes. He could see compassion in them. These men were not here to cause harm. He had a sense of these things.

"Lupe?" Mark said quietly, calmly….

"The man that took your friend, what did he look like?" she raised her head, as he handed her a tissue.

"Was he strange looking? White, pale? With pink eyes?"

"No he was tall and thin, blond and his eyes were blue. He had a tattoo of a Snake and a rainbow on his arm." She blew her nose. A leaf fell out of her hair and landed on the table. Lupe picked it up and studied it.

Mark sighed. It wasn't the Albino, but he was sure it was all tied in. The phone rang in the corner of the room.

Redbird picked up the receiver. "Yes?"

He hung up the phone without another word. He stood and opened the small door. Seraphine entered the room and walked over to Lupe.

Mark and Tom starred at each other.

"What the hell is this?" Mark whispered to Tom. He could feel chills running up his arms. It was the woman from the hotel.

Seraphine turned to Mark. "Where is your wife? I must speak with her."

She explained her connection to Lupe, and told him that she had another vision.

"Your daughter is alive. But time is running out."

Tom explained the cult angle and why they were here. Redbird had been involved in the investigation, looking for a single killer. It had hit home, with the Tribal council, because all the victims were Indians.

Tom filled Redbird in on the possible link to the cult, and although the killer may not be directly affiliated there was a link. He was sure of it.

This time Mark made haste. They loaded up in the truck, and Redbird followed them in his van.

When Raven opened her eyes they were crusted together, and her head hurt.

She was stretched out on a small bed.

Someone had covered her, and left a small lamp on low. The room was yellow and besides the bed and a nightstand there was nothing. She felt under the covers, to make sure her clothes were on. Panic rising in her chest.

Her head hurt worse trying to remember what had happened. Raven thought back to the events of the night. They had left the club and drove to get food. She had, had eggs and bacon and then...they had walked outside.

There had been a man....instinctively she touched her hand to her neck, he had put a knife to her throat, and suddenly it all came back to her. She had screamed for Lupe to run. There was a struggle and that was all she could remember. Had someone saved her and brought her to their house? She had no idea where she was, or how long she had been there.

Pushing herself up on one elbow and rubbing her eyes. Everything seemed to be working.

She threw the blanket off.

There didn't seem to be anything wrong with her. Once Raven was sure there were no injuries she swung her legs over the side of the bed. The floor was cold. Her shoes were gone. Probably lost in the struggle.

At first she was a little wobbly but Raven managed to stand up, and took the few steps across the room to reach the door.

She turned the knob and to her surprise it opened easily. Light filled the room, instinctively her hand went up to block the light.

Making her way down the small hallway, she hesitated after a few steps.

This could be the house of the man who attacked her. Raven knew she had to be careful.

"Your awake." The voice came from the thin blond woman sitting at a table.

She was older, in her fifties at least. Her hair was long, shoulder length, with grey streaks. Her face drawn, and thin.

"Come sit." She said, pointing to the empty chair.

Raven walked into the room and sat down opposite the woman.

"Well now, aren't you a sight for sore eyes." The woman said.

"Why am I here?" Raven asked.

"That is the question of the day isn't it?" the woman replied. She smiled a frail smile. Her thin hair hung loosely around her face. She didn't look like much of a threat. She looked like someone that had been sick for a long time. Her cheek bones were sunken, dark circles under her eyes.

"Could you please tell me why I'm here…" Raven asked quietly.

"I like that, you have respect. I am Anita, and you are here because of this."

She held up her grandmother's necklace.

"It's my Grandmas Necklace, she gave it to me before she died. I didn't steal it, I swear." Raven replied.

Anita laughed.

"Silly girl no one thinks you stole it. What was your Grandmother's name?"

"Isabella Moretti."

"Isabella…..your grandfather was Giovanni."

"Yes", Raven replied, with a hint of excitement, did you know them?"

"Yes, I knew them well." My father and your grandfather were colleagues of a sort."

"A man attacked me and my friend." Raven blurted out.

"Yes I apologize for that. He had no idea that you were under shade."

She saw the puzzled look on the girls face.

Meaning you are to be protected by this." She held out the amulet to Raven.

Taking the necklace she placed it over her head, and tucked it into her shirt.

"Thank you. It's all I have left of her."
"Loyal too, I like it…. Now, George, get your ass out here."
Raven starred as the man who attacked her walked into the kitchen. Her heart pounded in her chest, she was fearful of what would happen next. She slid back her chair and stood.

"Easy girl. He's not going to hurt you."

George lowered his eyes as he stood in front of her.

Her mouth went dry, and she felt like vomiting.

"I am sorry priestess. I had no idea she was shaded. As soon as I saw the necklace I stopped." Anita looked him up and down.

"I believe you, but you owe this young lady an apology."

He turned to her and bowed. "I am sorry." The tall blond man bowed, but his piercing blue eyes never lost contact with hers. There was no sincerity in the apology.

Raven sat down, her legs felt as heavy as stone. This was the weirdest thing that had ever happened to her. She still didn't feel safe. What kind of crazy shit was this? These people didn't look normal.

He had called her priestess. What the hell. Were they acting out some kind of creepy fantasy? She had seen a lot of wierdos in the last year. Surely these people were no exception.

Anita rang a small bell and a red headed girl entered the room. She wore a simple robe.

"Misha, bring food and drink." Misha bowed and left quickly, returning moments later with what appeared to be pot roast and potatoes, and large glass of milk.

Immediately Raven felt her stomach growling. Anita starred at her. "Eat girl."

Raven ate, and didn't feel George's ice cold eyes staring at her. He was furious. Losing the other girl, he now wanted to kill her. Anita watched him closely.

He could barely contain his disgust with her, as their eyes met. George was afraid of her, but this angered him, overshadowing all fear.

He averted his eyes when Anita spoke to him.

"You may leave, George. Remember the code. She is NOT yours."

"I understand." He answered, tilting his head to the side, as his blood boiled.

"Good. You may go." She shooed him away, like a fly.

"Since your grandmother and grandfather were high standing members of my church, it is expected that you also join and become one of us." Anita walked to the shelf, opening a cupboard.

"Read this…." She pushed a red book across the table toward Raven. "This is what we stand for and what we are about. We are your family now."

She crossed the room, lingering in the doorway.

"You are no longer alone, in the world. The book is your bible. Follow that always, and you will never go wrong. This is your home now. There is nothing to worry about. We care for each other and are like family."

Raven watched her. She was lost in her thoughts.

"I know this all seems unusual now and I'm sure you have many questions. All in good time. First eat, and rest, then we will get you some clothes and whatever you need." Anita's voice was soft and soothing.

Raven had been lonely for so long, and she missed Granny so much.

She had always coddled her and taken care of her. It felt good to belong. Anita sat with Raven, as she ate two plates of food. Afterwards they took a short walk in the garden, and Raven gave her a quick history of her life, Granny's death and the things that had transpired since.

She was easy to talk to and she really listened. It made her relax. "I understand your pain." Anita stated, patting her arm as they headed back toward the house. Raven saw George in the window as they walked by. He starred at her.

"Don't worry about the man," Anita said, taking Ravens hand.

"He works for me and he had no idea who you were. It will never happen again. As long as you are here you are safe."

Raven felt groggy. She needed to lie down. He brain was full of fog. Maybe there had been something in the food. Anita steered her back to her room, and tucked her into the bed. There was no time to watch her today. Once she was sure the medicine had worked, she left the room.

She had other things to do. Mitch would be assigned to the doorway, until she could be sure George was going to behave himself. He normally didn't act up like this.

She would be having another talk with him soon. The church was back up and running. New members were coming from Texas soon, and she had no time for foolishness, there were too many other things she had to complete this week.

Francis had been acting up a little, and she knew he was getting ready to cycle again. It was ridiculous. She shook her head. He was starting to tire her.

People were all pathetic to her. Anita kept the ones she could control. The rest she had no use for.

All she waited for now was the solstice. The sweet day, when she would be the most powerful woman on earth. The predictions were all coming true.

Grey heard the truck before it came down the drive.

"They are coming back." He said.

Megan put the sleeping child into his crib, and covered him. Noticing how tall he had gotten, wondering how tall Josephine was. Tears filled her eyes. She wiped them quickly. She was not going to do this today. Shutting the door, she joined Grey in the kitchen.

Megan sat down at the wooden table, and folded her hands.

"Looks like we have company." Grey stated as he watched a second vehicle pull down the drive.

He walked over to the fireplace and grabbed the shotgun, cocking it with one hand, as he pulled the 9mm out of his waistband with the other.

Watching the large Indian and a girl exit the truck, he cocked his head.

He froze in place as Seraphine exited the vehicle. Megan saw him tense up. She had spent enough time with him to know when his feathers were ruffled. She tried to see past him, but the door opened and Mark stepped inside. He looked flustered too.

Megan prayed it was not bad news. He was followed by Redbird and Lupe, and Tom......lastly, Seraphine entered the room.

Megan starred at her. "It's you...you were at the hotel."

"Yes." She smiled at Megan, as Mark directed her to the table. Once everyone was seated, Tom spoke.

"As you all know, the cult has resurfaced, not far from here. Just across the border. There have also been a series of murders here, all women, all Native American.

We believe that there is a single serial killer, but we have strong indication, that he is also linked to the cult." He filled Megan and Grey in on what had happened to Lupe and Raven.

Megan's throat went dry. She walked over to the sink and poured herself a glass of water. After taking a few sips, she returned to where Seraphine was sitting.

"You said my daughter was alive."

"Yes she lives, but I have no other vision of her at this time." She explained that her visions were scattered. They came at Random. She patted Megan's hand.

 "I wish I knew more, but I don't."

Lupe lay down in one of the bedrooms. Megan tucked her in. She felt sorry for the girl. She had been terrorized and nearly killed.

"You rest." She said kindly. Seraphine kissed Lupe on the forehead.

"Don't worry little one. You are safe here."

The men discussed the cult, and Megan returned to the kitchen, just in time to hear Redbird stating that he had heard of this group, and had all his information from the FBI, and as of late, it had not been officially linked, to the disappearance of the girls.

The FBI had profiled a single serial killer. Tom disagreed, but had been told by his superior to focus on the murders, and leave the cult angle alone.

Redbird agreed that they were connected, in some way. THE Council had not heard of the cult, just that one Girl after another was disappearing. Three had disappeared from the club, and there could be many more victims, he suspected.

Now they had a description of the killer. Hopefully it would bring some more leads. Redbird had heard rumors in town, of a new church group in the area, with ties to Satanism, and sacrifices. There was nothing concrete though.

Megan starred at Seraphine.

"Lupe's friend, her name is Raven."

"Yes."

"Is she the one you spoke of?"

"She is." Seraphine sat down on the chair next to Megan.

"How is she important? Does she know where my daughter is?"

Megan was getting worked up. Mark put his hand protectively around her shoulders.

"Babe, calm down let her speak...." He said softly.

Seraphine closed her eyes.....concentrating. The vision was faint.

"The Raven is coming into her own. She does not know herself, just yet. I do not see your child at this time."

"Does that mean something has happened to her?" Megan was quickly becoming hysterical.

Seraphine leaned forward and placed her hand on Megan's.

"I cannot see her at this time. I do not feel like she has been harmed. Be patient all will be revealed soon."

Seraphine's touch somehow calmed her.

Tom and redbird would make sure the composite sketch got out to all the agencies, and Redbird would distribute it among his people. It was a start.

Grey decided to head to the station with Tom, while Redbird, Lupe and Seraphine went to meet with the tribal council.

Mark finished his coffee and checked on the Sam. He slept, dreaming a child's dreams.....

He walked up behind Megan and wrapped his arms around her. He kissed her neck and pulled her closer.

"I love you. We are going to find her."

"I believe that." She replied.

"I'm sorry I wasn't there for you. I failed you. I lost my edge, and let all this happen." Tears formed in his eyes. He had finally said what he had been thinking for all these months.

Megan turned to him.

"This is not your fault. You almost died protecting me. More than once. I know you did everything you could."

"It wasn't enough." He shook his head, his guilt heavy in his heart.

"No. It was enough. We will get her back. I can feel it. This whole thing started with my family, not you. You came along and risked your life for me, when you didn't have to. You could have just walked away, but you stayed."

She took his hand in hers. "Grey told me that you were going to kill yourself."

Mark sat down on the bed next to Megan. He hadn't seen this coming. He swallowed hard. He never wanted her to know that part of him. The dark part.

He spoke freely now. She knew, and somehow he needed to get it out once and for all.

"I wanted to. I thought you and the baby might be dead. I searched for you everywhere. There was nothing.

Then, when the cult disbanded they killed a lot of people. All the lower standing members were murdered, to keep them from talking. Their bodies were thrown into mass graves.

Tom found me in the hospital, and took me to the digs. There were bags of bodies already excavated, and some had photos pinned to them, that were already catalogued. The rest, I dug through myself.

Every bag I unzipped, was fucking hell. I was looking for you, and praying I wouldn't find you." He shook his head, remembering. A large lump had formed in his throat.

"I searched and searched and there was nothing. No trace, no shred of life.

So, finally I went home, back to the cabin where we started. It was the one place I could still feel you, and then even that went away. I couldn't feel anything.

All I could see was darkness. So I decided to do it. I downed a bottle of Jim beam, pulled the trigger, and the 9mm jammed. That was that." He said matter of factly. Mark sat, leaning over, with his hands clasped in his lap.

Megan didn't like the look in his eyes...it made her uncomfortable.

"Babe.....we're ok. I'm here now. I didn't know."

She had no idea what he had been through. The idea of him digging through corpses to look for her was a thought she couldn't even begin to wrap her mind around.

"None of this is your fault. We are dealing with things out of our control." she said gently. Grey had not given her all these details, and she felt grateful to have a man that loved her that much. She thanked God silently for sparing him, by making the gun jam.

"Someday this will end, and we will get our lives back." Megan said. She put her arms around him and held him. Moments later he took her face in his hands and kissed her.

"I won't fail you again." He said as he stood and walked out of the room.

Megan knew that he was still stuck in the past, and that he blamed himself, and nothing she said to him had sunk in. She prayed he could somehow get past it.

That night as she had the last week, she ate by herself, bathed and tucked Sam in, and went to bed alone.

When tom and Grey returned Mark walked out the door, right past them and without saying a word got into his truck and drove away.

He was pissed at Grey for telling her, but he knew he was trying to help. Grey always thought he understood what he was going through, and in some ways it was the same, but it was also different.

He had found his family dead in the snow. He buried them.

Mark had almost lost his mind searching, when the trail went deader than dead.

Then the bodies, the rotting decomposing flesh that he had to look through, to find the one person, the only person he had ever loved. The woman who believed in him, and completed him and the child she was carrying, inside her.

There was no greater torture, until his daughter had been stolen from him, and again, he was losing everything he loved.

Mark drove through the night. He needed some time to get himself together, before he went completely crazy. He felt like he was right on the edge teetering back and forth. The music blared on the radio. Sometimes he could get his mind together easier if there was outside noise. He didn't do well with quiet. He had had too much of that in his life.

He longed for a house filled with children, their footsteps running through the house. He pictured a dog barking and toys scattered about. That was all he wanted to grow old with his family and end this nightmare.

He wanted to hit someone, anyone. Maybe he would find a bar, and pick a fight. Mark drove on into the night.

In the morning Megan woke early. Sam slept. She walked into the kitchen, checking the window to see if Mark had returned.

"He's not back." Grey said, handing her a cup of coffee.

"What happened? You two have a fight?" Grey asked in his deep drawl.

"No. He is blaming himself, for everything. He's really struggling with it. I can't seem help him. I told him that I don't blame him, and I don't, but he isn't hearing me at all. I told him that you told me, that he tried to kill himself." Grey nodded his head.

"He's got a ghost on him."

Anita stopped George as he walked down the hall.

"Let me ask you something" she said.

"I see how you look at Raven. You do understand what the rules are here don't you?"

George stopped in his tracks. He starred at his feet for a moment.

"The rules?" his jaw tightened. They had already discussed it. He didn't understand why she was bringing it up again.

"Yes, I like her and I am keeping her here. She is protected. You will NOT touch her, are we clear?" her tone suggested that she was wanting to start a fight with him.

"Yes I know the rules." He wasn't playing into that, because she would have the guards on him in a heartbeat. He gritted his teeth.

"Just be sure you don't forget them." She said tauntingly, smiling and stroking his face.

"Of course, you could make it up to me." She whispered, in his ear. Bile rose in his throat. He clenched his fists. He felt his pulse began to rise. His ice blue eyes staring straight ahead.

"Well that's ok...." She sneered.

"You know what the punishment is. "Don't cross that line."

He counted his breaths. It was a safety mechanism he used to calm himself when needed. She was pissed, that he wouldn't fuck her. She had tried him, the first few days he had been in the compound. She wasn't his type then, and nothing had changed. He was the one who controlled things, not her.

At first he liked being part of the church as she liked to call it. Now he was tired of the whole thing. It was a joke. Anita made and changed the rules as she pleased.

He breathed deeply and counted his heartbeat, in his mind.

"I get it" He finally said. The reply was nothing more than a hiss. Now he understood why she was treating him this way, after all he had done for her, and for the cult. She was jealous and pissed at him, for wanting Raven. He had seen her going into the cell, and letting Francis fuck her. It disgusted him. Not only was she not his type, but he couldn't stand the sight of her anymore.

It was unacceptable. He didn't like to be disrespected by any women. In his opinion they were good for nothing, except killing, and George had been killing since he was a child.

First it was the family pet, then the neighborhood pets, and once he had killed the preacher's poodle from down the street.

The poor thing had made its way to him. The small pink bell on the collar had alerted him of Fluffy's presence.

He lured it into the back yard with a pork chop that his mother had left on the stove.

Once the dog started eating, he had bashed his head with a baseball bat, over and over, until there was no sound or movement left.

He gutted the dog, unsure if it was alive or dead. He wanted to understand how things worked. Holding the bloody organs in his hands gave him a sense of accomplishment.

Later he studied medical journals and learned every surgical technique, yet his weapon of choice continued to be his hands, strangulation, he loved to watch the life ebb out of their body, as he squeezed their necks. His serrated knife was also a favorite choice. He liked the way skin sounded when it was sliced.

It made him feel like a man, and aroused him to no end.

The blank stare that they had the moment their life left them. The life he had squeezed from them, or bled from them. That was what really turned him on. It surged a power through him like nothing else.

George was a sociopath and had been one since birth.

Anita addressed George again.

"Are you listening?" It brought him back to the moment.

"Yes." He turned and starred at her, making eye contact.

"I don't want any mistakes." She stated. He starred at her.

"I'm not the one who slips up." George replied quietly.

She knew he was referring to Francis. It was true. On more than one occasion since they had been in New Mexico she had to clean up after the Albino's rampage. His impulses were getting worse and closer together.

The bloody scenes were getting harder and harder to cover up. She had become afraid of him. He couldn't be controlled. He was a liability. Anita would never tell anyone of her fear of Francis, but he was the main reason she had hired George.

One prostitute after the other, each more gruesome than the last. Each scene Impossible to hide. He had no restraint. He could no longer be trusted. Just the previous night, he had killed Misha. He had spread her legs so wide they had split.

Her bloody body thrown down the basement steps. Now, there was no one to do the damn cooking.

She could imagine how he had spread her apart. He was so large, that Anita didn't visit him often, but she would have to pay him a visit soon. Sometimes she liked the pain of it. She liked the pain.

He had attacked Misha from behind, as she cooked dinner, slamming her face onto the hot burner. He had raped her, forcing his massive body onto hers.

The guards had him at gunpoint when Anita came into the room, but it was too late. Although Misha's screams had initially brought them running, but in the few seconds it took to get there, he had already ripped her innards to shreds, and thrown her lifeless body away.

They guards didn't like to deal with Francis. He was unpredictable, and like a wild animal when he was on a rampage.

Misha had been one of his cleaner kills, but he was losing control all the same. He knew people in the house were off limits. Anita couldn't let him out. Now she couldn't trust him in the house. He would have to go back into the cage.

It wasn't the killing that bothered her. She didn't give a damn about them. They were nothing to her.

It was his rage that was out of control. He would have sex with them and the sheer size of him would send them screaming, those screams were what set him off. He killed to quiet them.

So she had hired George. He was her ace in the hole. It was the only way she felt safe. Knowing what George did, Gave her a strange comfort. He was a calculated killer. It she wanted Francis gone George would make it happen.

She had watched him for months. It was one of the reasons she had hired him. Anita was in need of someone without a conscience, but unlike Francis, he cleaned up his mess.

He killed and tidied up. George wasn't a rage killer. Even the clean- up made him feel good. It excited him. It was like an aphrodisiac. The problem was that the high never lasted long.

George left no evidence, unlike the Albino. Who left a trail of bloody destruction, everywhere he went.

Anita knew if she didn't get Francis under control, George would. It was what they had discussed at the beginning. He would not disobey her.

But George was pissed. She could tell by the look on his face, but to Anita the church rules were written in stone. It was black and white.

She never deviated from the rules. George would get over it. She was sure.

Raven was protected. She would not let him have her.

She had plans for Raven. Plans that would take them to new heights. Raven was loyal, and she needed someone like her, to be her companion.

She had grown weary of being alone.

Anita had the child, and with her, she would become the most powerful priestess of all time. It was true she felt slightly sorry for the little thing, but she would help her ascend, and that was the way of it.

All was fair in war, and this was surely a war. There were always casualties.

George faced her head on. "Are we done here?"

"Yes." The chilly voice replied.

His rage was boiling over. He couldn't stand to be told what to do. Now she was taking something from him. He wanted Raven. Granted she wasn't his first choice, but he would have her. Not to keep her. George had been watching her for the last few days. The way the veins in her neck stood out.

He wanted to squeeze the life out of her. Every time he thought of it, he became hard. He didn't understand it. She wasn't his type at all.

Regardless, he always took what he wanted. He especially wanted the things he couldn't have. He would have the other bitch too. All in good time.

The one that got away would be his soon too.

In a way it amused him. He had never had an escapee. The chase would be ten times sweeter than the first time.

George could wait.

He was a patient man.

He would find her, and just for the aggravation he would kill her entire family, watch their miserable lives drain out of them too.

His rage had now turned to lust.

He walked into his room, aroused, thinking of all the killing he would soon be able to do. He rubbed himself just the way he liked it.

Fuck Anita, he thought.

No one would tell him what to do. Not even her. He reached into his pants and grabbed his shaft. He pictured strangling Raven. It made him come quickly.

Afterwards, he did not feel satisfied.

It had to be soon. He would have to go to the city and find a girl.

George wouldn't kill tonight though he didn't want to draw any attention to himself. He was a private person. All the distention with Anita had already thrown off his equilibrium.

He had a much better plan, one that would piss Anita off, and make him look like a saint. After all he aimed to please.

Francis paced the cage for hours. He had defecated on himself and was walking through it. He chanted late into the night, and beat himself with a chain across his back as he paced knowing Anita was angry with him. He couldn't help it. He needed the girls.

The priestess didn't understand. She had left him again. Caged like an animal.

Abandoned him like everyone else. So he paced back and forth back and forth...rattling the iron cage with his sheer size.

He refused to eat or drink. He knew eventually she would come for him.

As soon as she did, she would take him to the city, to find another girl.

Francis often thought of Megan and the way her panties smelled when he had stolen them from the Mansion. Every woman he killed was Megan. He was driven by need and lust. Nothing else mattered.

For years he had fantasized over her picture that Anita had given him, promising him that before she ascended, he could have her for just one night. It had grown into an obsession. A want that drove him on, killing and maiming until he could have the one he wanted.

Francis heard the door to the cellar creaking open. He knew she had come for him, finally.

When the figure came into the light, he was disappointed at the sight of George.

"Hey buddy, how's it going?" he said lightly. George leaned at the foot of the stairs His hands in his pockets leisurely.

He wore jeans and a white and blue shirt. The smell was foul. It took everything George had to keep the smile on his face, and not wrinkle his nose.

"I see she's got you locked up again."

"She will come for me." Francis said as he stopped pacing.

"No, doesn't look like it to me. She hasn't come for you in a couple of days."

"She will." The large figure whispered. He pressed his large face into the bars and closed his eyes.

"Buddy she is not coming for you tonight. Don't you want to go out and have some fun?"

"The priestess said I'm not allowed out. I was bad, and I'm being punished."

He reminded George of the man from mice and men. The one that was slow.

"Oh well, we could go have a little fun. She will never know." George said the magic words.

"We can find a girl."

"I can't get out the door is locked." His excitement was evident now. His pink eyes sparkled eerily making his pale face look even more ominous than usual.

He rattled the gate with his massive hands, starring at the padlock.

"Well I don't know about that." George pulled a key ring out of his pocket.

"What do you say, you wanna go for a ride in the van?'

"Yes I do, and find a girl?"

"Absolutely." George slipped the key into the lock and it turned and made a loud clicking sound. The heavy rod iron door creaked open, and Francis ducked down to step out. George locked the door back and smiled in delight as it clicked again.

It amused George to picture the guard's faces in the morning, knowing he was on the loose. They would be shitting themselves. He could imagine them checking every crack and crevice of the house.

He smiled and hung the key ring back on the hook at the top of the stairs. The hallway was dark, as they entered it.

The guards had bigger fish to fry. No one went near Francis.

Francis followed him like a puppy.

"Where are we going George?"

"To take a damn bath, now be quiet." He commanded.

He took Francis to the guest room, and locked the door. He left him in the large shower with a bottle of body soap, and told him to wash everything, and keep washing till he came back with some clothes.

No one saw him load Francis into the van. He even came back inside and made sure the Guards saw him leave, alone. That would only sweeten the pot. He chuckled to himself as the vehicle rolled through the city.

Finally after what seemed like hours, and countless questions by Francis, he found the place he was looking for.

George steered them to the seedy part of town, where he knew even a freak like Francis would be able to find a girl.

The Albino waited in the van while George found a girl.

The prostitute entered the van where Francis was waiting. George had paid her fifty dollars, and had reiterated that he was unusually large, in the penis department, and not much to look at.

Granted he looked better in street clothes than those creep ass robes, but still he looked like a giant freak of nature. George had found pants and a shirt for him, which was no small feat considering his massive size.

She stepped inside the van. George pulled the curtain and drove.

The sounds were familiar. Then as he pulled onto the highway the screaming began.

Once everything went quiet, he pulled back into town, and found a pay phone, called 911 and reported a murder.

George dumped the bloody mangled prostitute onto the sidewalk. He wasn't able to contain the smile on his face, when Francis jumped out, and kneeled down next to her, cradling the lifeless body in his arms. He wasn't giving her up. She belonged to him.

George drove away with a twinkle in his eyes. This was just the beginning.

"You take from me, I take from you." he said to himself.

Raven had been with Anita for a few weeks now. She was treated well. Anita felt a connection to her.

She was the companion she never had. Anita liked her mind, and as far as her family was concerned she came from old loyal ties.

Their conversations flowed freely, and Anita loved hearing Raven's stories from the club. Most of all she liked looking at her while she spoke.

The curve of her lips and the way her long hair hung loosely over her shoulders. Sometimes if Raven moved a certain way Anita caught a whiff of the way her hair smelled.

After a long night of stripper stories and a bottle of whiskey Anita had asked Raven to dance for her. Although Raven thought it awkward she complied. If she had caught on to one thing, it was that you didn't say no to Anita.

Anita watched Ravens slender, but curvy body dance... She wanted to understand what she was feeling. She had never been attracted to a woman, it was awkward at best.

Her emotions were slipping away from her....Anita didn't like to be out of control, but this was something new. It made her nervous.

Nervous but excited. She hadn't said anything to Raven, but she longed to touch her.

Raven avoided her as much as possible. She wanted to go home. She had asked Anita about it, and had simply been put off about it. She was a prisoner no matter how you cut it.

Raven had witnessed a ceremony in the great room. Men in Robes were chanting and Anita stood in the middle of them naked. She had retreated back into her room quickly. Her heart pounding. They had all worn the same pendant. Just like the one Granny had given her.

She had to get out of here. Raven wanted no part of this freak show.

Anita had thought about Raven for days. She decided the best thing was for her to put Raven with the kid. She would be able to kill three birds with one stone.

It would keep her out of George's sight, and she knew Raven would be loyal. It would get her mind off of her body, and stop the crazy fantasies she was having about her. Anita had been up for a few nights masturbating and thinking of her.

She needed to get some sleep, before the men from Texas came. After that, she would have her dance for her again, and then she would do whatever she wanted, to Raven.

She did belong to her now.

She could smell her scent, when she walked by, and wanted to do things to her that she had never thought of.

George watched from the shadows. Once Anita was gone and Raven was alone at the table, he stepped out.

"She's never going to let you go. After she kills that little girl, she will kill you too."

Raven starred at him, but didn't answer. She had no idea what the hell he was talking about. There was no little girl. Raven was confused. Was he trying to help her? She knew if he was it was for his own Agenda. He stepped back into the darkness of the hallway and disappeared into his room.

The next morning Anita met with Raven for breakfast.

Anita brushed her hair away from her face and felt that strange twinge again. She was wearing the sexy pink tank top that she had bought her. She had asked her to wear it today.

Anita discussed the cult and the general rules with Raven again. Although she had never known about her family connections, she listened intently.

Raven needed to find out what was really going on. Her feelings of belonging had left her, and an ominous feeling had settled instead. Still she wanted to know what Granny had been part of. Had she been a willing participant, or had grandpa made her do it.

She could feel Anita leaning in closer. It made her a little uncomfortable but she had gotten used to it, in the strip club. Men loved to lean in close and touch her. She didn't like it, but just like then, she kept a smile on her face. It was a means to an end.

One they finished discussing the book Anita asked Raven to follow her and they walked down a long hallway together, and turned right, down another corridor. It seemed to slope downhill and at the bottom there was a heavy iron door with a guard that led to a set of steps.

 At the bottom, was another Guard.

"Open it." Anita commanded.

Greg unlocked the heavy metal door, and pulled it open. It was a large room, containing a dilapidated toddler bed, with a small child sitting on it. In the corner there was a small petition, housing a bathroom, complete with a walk in shower, a washing machine, and utility sink.

This must have been the child that George had talked about.

"Leave us." She instructed the guard, who still lingered in the doorway.

She starred at the two women with big wide eyes, but never uttered a sound.

"Hi." Raven said. Putting her hand up, in a waving gesture. The smell in the room was atrocious.

Anita explained that she wanted Raven to stay with the girl, and be her caregiver.

"I'm no good with kids. I'm a stripper for god's sake." Raven whined.

Anita laughed. "It's ok you can learn. She is very well behaved, and she doesn't speak."

"She doesn't talk at all?" Raven inquired.

"No, not a word." Anita shrugged.

"Is there something wrong with her?"

"I don't know. She's never talked since she's been here."

"Don't they normally talk at this age?"

"She has never uttered a word. Maybe she is retarded." She said callously.

"Where did she come from?" Raven asked inquisitively.

"She is my granddaughter."

"Oh", Raven replied. Why do you keep her locked up down here?"

"She is very important to me, and I don't want anything to happen to her." Anita replied waving her hand to dismiss any further questions.

"Oh," Raven said. Wondering what kind of sick game they were playing.

They stood and watched the child, who had obviously been abandoned by the state of the room.

Anita didn't seem to notice, and was too busy watching Raven. The Pink tank top she had brought her, showed off her breasts.

She couldn't wait to ascend. Just the thought of that glorious night made her heart pound faster. It would be the glory of all glories, and the dark lord would be so proud. Then she could have anyone she wanted.

Raven turned around and Anita blushed.

She looked towards the girl again, while a very uncomfortable feeling washed over her. Raven knew this was a bad and dangerous situation.

"So what are you protecting her from? And, does she have a name?"

"No, no name …" Anita replied.

"It's better that way."

That didn't sound right at all. She would have to fish around some more.

"Wouldn't you want to keep her with you?"

"No...." Anita stated quickly.

"Enough with the questions." She said sternly.

Raven didn't want to push the issue.

"Ok I'll stay with her." She felt like it was what she was supposed to do.

"Great. I'll have the guards bring you the things that you need. I will have a TV and movies sent down and the little window in the door opens, and you can ask the guard for anything that you want."

"What, you want me to stay now?" Raven asked in disbelief.

"Yes. I'll see you in a few days." Anita said as she left the room, leaving Raven starring after her in astonishment. The door shut and Raven heard the key turn the lock.

Anita briefly spoke to Greg the guard outside. "Get her whatever she needs, and don't let them out of your sight. No one leaves this room, and if George comes near her shoot him."

Greg nodded. He had waited all day to see who was coming. Anita had told them she would be bringing in someone to watch the girl.

Since the Albino had killed Misha there was no one to care for her, and the whole thing was getting on his nerves. It was stupid to guard a child that didn't talk, and couldn't get out. It was boring as fuck. He didn't like the part about George.

No one here liked to fuck with him. He was a cold bastard that would be behind you, slicing your throat, before you even knew it. Greg was glad he was at the bottom of the steps, at least he would be able to see him coming.

Raven looked around. It was obvious no one had been here, except to drop off food in many days.

There were dirty bowls all over the floor, and the little girls face and clothes were covered in food, dirt and grime.

Raven banged on the door with both fists.

"What?" Greg asked in annoyance.

"Bring me some towels, and some kind of cleaner. Preferably bleach, laundry soap, baby soap, whatever a kid can use, and take these dirty bowls out of here. Oh, and we need dinner."

Two hours later Raven had cleaned all the feces and urine, off the floor. Luckily it was localized to the back of the room. The little girl couldn't have been more than two or three. She was blond and blue eyed.

She stripped the beds, and washed down the child's mattress. In the small dresser she found a larger sheet, but managed to tuck it under. She coaxed the girl off the floor and into the bathroom.

"I'm Raven." She said lightly.

"You really need a bath. I am not going to hurt you."

She waved her over, and to her surprise, she came and let her pull the soiled dress over her head. She reeked. Her hair was matted to her head. It must have been weeks since she had a bath.

Raven turned on the water. Once she was satisfied that it wasn't too hot or too cold, she moved the small body into the shower, and washed her. Her hair had to be washed twice. Raven studied the birthmark on the back of her neck. It looked like a circle in a circle. It was unusual. She dreaded combing out the matted hair.

Raven dried her, and put clean pajamas on her. Greg came back with roasted chicken and mashed potatoes, and green beans.

She made a bowl for the child. They sat on the floor and ate.

"You need a name." Raven told her. The girl looked up at her as she stuffed food in with both hands.

"Don't worry. I'm not going to leave you."

After dinner she cleaned the child up again. At 8 pm both beds were made up, the clothes were done and folded, and the child slept. Raven had to figure out a way to get out of here. Something really crazy was going on here. Maybe they had kidnapped the kid, and were holding her for ransom. She would find out, one way or another.

It was after ten when George sauntered down the steps.

Greg pulled his gun. "You know you're not supposed to be here." He said in a shaky voice. "I have orders to shoot you."

George smiled, and continued down the steps. "We both know you aren't going to shoot me, besides all I want to do is talk to her. Mitch said it's ok."

Greg yelled upstairs.

"MITCH"

The door opened and Mitch peered down the stairs.

"Fuck dude I thought you were dead."

"Gentlemen, what kind of despicable man do you take me for?" He clutched his chest dramatically.

"Let him talk to her."

Greg stepped aside, as George slid open the window.

Raven saw him, and came closer.

"Hi." George said, with a smile.

"What do you want?"

"Just a friendly piece of advice. Everyone here wants to kill you, and the kid."

She interrupted him.

"Why?"

"Well, I want to kill you because it's your fault that I couldn't kill Lupe."

"Why does she want to kill the kid?" Raven asked, ignoring his last statement.

"It's a sacrifice. So she can become more powerful. She will kill both of you if she gets the chance."

"Why are you even telling me this?"

"I don't know." He said.

"I guess I'm trying to be a good guy. I feel sorry for the kid."

"I'll make you a deal. If I help you get out of here, with the kid, you come back, and well...you know what comes next. I promise to let you live till she is safe. It's a fair trade you, for her. If you don't come back I will find you both and kill you slowly." He smiled sweetly.

"I'll think about it." Raven said sarcastically.

"Why does she need her?"

"She is the next, direct descendant of the blood line."

"What is this god that they keep referring to in the Manual."

"Well...it's the devil honey." He smiled sweetly.

The door at the top of the stairs opened.

"She's back." Mitch whispered.

George closed the window, and headed up the stairs. By the time Anita came inside he was in his room. It was true he did feel sorry for the kid in a way. He didn't really know why he went down to the basement to tell Raven.

He was bored, and he wanted to see if she would give her life for the kids. It amused him that she would. He was sure she would hold to her word and come back. Even if she didn't he would just hunt them both down.

Then he wouldn't have to feel any guilt about the kid, because it would be Raven's fault, not his.

Raven sat back down on the bed. She had to find a way to get out of here, or she would have no choice, except to take George up on his offer.

Her life for the child's. She was ok with that. It was despicable to leave a child alone like this. George was probably right. It made her nervous. Yet she had a feeling that everything he said was true.

Something wasn't right with this whole situation. Why did George say that Anita was going to kill the child? She was not a direct descendant.

The direct one would have been her Mother. It just didn't make sense. She had to read her manual. She was sure that the ascention was part of it, and the more she read the sicker she felt.

The church of the followers of the Divine Rainbow, was nothing more than a cult.

Anita was the high priestess and the dark lord that they spoke of in their bible, was the devil himself. George had confirmed it. It scared Raven to think of the Devil. She was a believer and had read her bible front to back. She knew the devil was nothing to play around with.

She would pray tonight, that they would be able to get out of here safely, and thank god that she had gotten this far, and been able to find the child. Maybe this was the thing the old man in the dream had referred to, maybe this was the thing she was supposed to do.

The ascention was harder to understand, but it went by bloodline. A pure one sacrificed, after the third birthday. She glanced over at the little girl. She couldn't be sure of her age, but it was close. Time was running out.

Somehow she knew.

Anita was planning on killing her own granddaughter, and now Raven was locked up in this dungeon with her.

The small window in the door slid open.

"You need anything?" Greg asked.

"No." Raven answered quickly.

He smiled. She could see the bottom row of his teeth had rotted completely. "Well if you need anything at all I'm at your service." he sneered. She was glad to hear the window close. He gave her the creeps.

She sat down in the rocking chair, lost in her thoughts. Once again the dream of the old man and the field flashed into her mind.

"You are not done here yet."

She couldn't quite wrap her mind around it, but this was like a de Ja vu. She was supposed to be here, although she didn't know why. It was her destiny. She supposed it was to save the child, as she had thought earlier.

Raven knocked on the window, and asked the Greg for pizza. He was short and skinny, with oily unkempt hair. He grinned, his rotten tooth grin.

"What's in it for me?"

He knew better than to touch her, but maybe after that stupid kid was gone he could get his hands on her. He would have to wait it out. He missed Misha.

She was so compliant. One look at his gun, she would get scared and lift her skirts.

He had threatened her several times and had gotten to get two blow jobs out of it, and had, had sex with her several times. He didn't even care that she had cried through the whole thing. He had enjoyed it.

"Well, what about the pizza?" Raven asked. It snapped him back into reality.

She had two reasons. Number one she wanted to see if she could really get whatever she wanted, whenever, and to know how close it was to town. She gave him story about the gluten in frozen pizza, and that she couldn't eat it.

 She went on about the cramping, and the diarrhea, he held up his hand to silence her, and yelled for Mitch.

It took 40 minutes for her to get Dominoes. So there had to be a town nearby. This would be good information for later. She settled into the rocker and continued to read the bound Bible that Anita had given her.

The rules and regulations of the church. Membership benefits, and responsibilities.

Raven wondered about Granny and pops. How had they become involved in this organization, and how had she not known. How had they managed to keep it from her all these years. It would at least explain why gramps had had such an aversion to the bible.

It was crazy. The ascension definitely involved a sacrifice. It would bring the person ascending great power. A power not of this earth.

The power of darkness.

A chill ran over her. She stood and stretched, trying to lose this feeling of impending doom, that had crept over her.

The window opened. Raven could hear the track sliding. She sat on the floor and did some stretches to ease her mind, and spirit.

Ever aware that Greg watched her every move. The child made small noises and thrashed in the bed. She woke up, as Raven picked her up and held her in her lap. First they starred at each other in silence.

Raven spoke sweetly to her, and got a small smile out of her. She must have had a bad dream.

She felt an instant connection. The little girl's eyes locked with hers. She was small for her age. She had never spoken a word since she had arrived here, yet she was able to walk. It was just odd.

Maybe no one had ever spoken to her.

"You need a name," she told her. "How about Josephine." Raven didn't know where the name came from, but she knew instinctively that it fit.

She gave her a cup of milk, and then sat her on the toilet. Raven clapped and danced when she peed in the toilet. Josephine gave her a crooked smile.

As the night got later, she rocked her to sleep, and put her in bed with her.

She didn't trust this place.

Raven was lost in her thoughts, her eyes heavy.

She started to doze off again, and suddenly she was back in the field.

This time a storm brewed and the man with the white beard stood. The wind blew his white hair and he looked angry. "You have to protect her. Evil forces are all around you now. Trust no one." His voice faded as he walked away. She could no longer make out his words.

"WHAT?" she shouted. The breeze had really picked up, and her hair was flying around her face. It howled now and she could barely make him out.

"What did you say? What do you want me to do?" Raven shouted into the wind, but the wind only howled louder and drowned out her voice.

When she woke up, she was back in the room in the small bed that had been provided for her.

The days went on. Raven and Josephine had a daily routine. They grew close in a short amount of time. Raven could tell that Josephine was smart. She would point when she wanted things, but still she would not utter a word.

 Raven spoke with Greg on several occasions, and put on a show for him when she knew he was watching her. It would come in handy later.

A week later Anita came and brought breakfast.

"How was your week?" she asked. Her hair was pulled back into a tight pony tail and her eyebrows had been freshly drawn on. She looked ridiculous. Raven wondered if she had, had some sort of mental breakdown. She looked haggard and worn. Her face not the same.

"Great." Raven lied cheerfully.

"I see you cleaned the place up." She couldn't stand still and flitted about.

The dark color of her eyebrows didn't match her blond hair. Her yellow pressed suit was no compliment either.

She looked odd, like she was in a kind of frenzy. She moved about nervously.

"Is everything ok?" Raven asked carefully.

"Yes…. Yes of course it is. How are things here?"

"Good. No problems. She is easy to take care of. We are getting to know each other."

"Well don't get too attached to her." Anita stated dryly.

"It won't be good for you in the long run."

Raven said nothing. She sat with her hands folded, knowing what it meant.

"Has she spoken?"

"No." Raven saw Josephine roll over towards the wall.

"Did you read the book that I gave you?"

"Yes."

"…and do you understand your responsibilities?"

"Yes."

"As a direct descendant of loyal followers you are grandfathered in so to speak. We will still have a ceremony, just not right now. I have some other pressing things that I need to take care of." Her eyes were icy.

She had found out that Francis had been arrested and was going to confront George about it. She was more than angry and worried that the Albino would talk to the police. He was slow after all and she couldn't trust him anymore.

This was not the time for this. There was too much going on. This arrest could compromise everything.

"Do you have any questions?" she asked matter of factly in a dismissive tone.

"Yes I didn't really understand the ascension part."

Anita's eyes glazed over.

"It is glorious." She whispered. Anita looked quite mad.

The ascension is a ceremony in which I will rise to the greatest power the power of my lord. We will all be a part of it."

She sat down next to Raven.

"I'm glad that you are here. I wished that my daughter Megan and I could have had this kind of relationship, but all she cared about was being with a man.

A disgusting man. She gave up everything for that, but now I don't need Megan anymore because I have her."

She stated, pointing at Josephine.

"What are you going to do with her?" Raven asked.

"She is going to help me ascend, and bring me to power. It will be the most glorious sacrifice to our lord that has ever taken place."

She smiled wickedly. Raven could feel her hair on her arms stand up.

Everything George had said was true.

She kept a smile plastered on her face, as Anita patted her leg.

"You mean you are going to use the girl as a sacrifice." she said softly, already knowing the answer.

"Yes!" Anita shouted jovially, clapping her hands together. You did read your manual. It will be the greatest moment of my life. You will be by my side Raven. And once I come into power we will stand together."

Raven's heart pounded. It took everything she had not to change her expression.

"What the fuck,".....those words seemed to be stuck in her brain.

She nodded and shook her head in agreeance, hoping that her false smile would not be detected. Anita closed her eyes and fantasized for a moment, then, she opened her eyes and stood up.

"I have pressing matters to attend to. Is there anything that you need?"

"Well I was wondering if I could go into town to shop, I really wanted to get some new clothes that I could wear for you, later....when we can be alone."

She wanted to get a glimpse of town and see where she was, and formulate some kind of plan to save herself and Josephine.

Raven had picked up on Anita's vibes from the other day. She saw the way she looked at her. She didn't mean a word of it, but if there was one thing that the strip club had taught her, it was how to be a hustler to get what she wanted.

She hadn't been like some of the other girls that had done anything for money. Raven would lap dance and maybe let one touch her for a moment if funds were low. But she learned what to say, and how to lie.

"Well she stays here." She pointed at Josephine.

"I know. I want to shop. I didn't want to take her. Do you think it will be ok?" she smiled and leaned closer to Anita. "I would be so grateful"

"I think that could be arranged." Anita smiled.

"It won't be for a few days though." She rubbed her hand across Ravens thigh. It made her skin crawl.

Raven jumped up and hugged Anita.

"Thank you so much." Anita smiled and hugged her back. She took in Ravens scent. It would be glorious.

The two of them together…., but she had bigger fish to fry right now. She stepped back and smoothed down her jacket. She couldn't lose her edge now.

"Alright, I will see you in a few days." Anita tapped on the door, and Greg let her out, locking up behind her. As soon as the lock clicked, Josephine rolled over, she stood and came to sit next to Raven on her bed, slipping her small hand in hers.

Raven looked at her. "I'm trying. I will get us out of here. When they let me out, you have to stay alone for just a little while. I have to see what's out there, and make a plan. I will come back for you though." Josephine nodded.

Raven knocked on the window. Greg's face came into view.

"What?"

"Tell George I need to talk to him." He starred at her for a moment and slammed the window. Raven smiled. She knew he was too afraid to not relay the message.

Anita headed down the corridor to the back yard where George waited with two of her Armed guards. As she walked out of the door, She stood tall and proud. Her painted on eyebrows glistening in the sun.

She was mad as a hatter. Her eyes cold, as she approached him.

"George…" She tilted her head and smiled, there was no love in it.

He starred at her coldly. His thin lips clamped tight. He was still angry with her, from the other day when she had openly scolded him.

Now, she had disturbed him. Dragging him out of his sleep, to bring him outside, knowing he hated it.

She faced him. Standing toe to toe.

"You took Francis without my permission." Shaking her head and sighing. She paced by him slowly. Her hands clasped behind her back.

Her head tilted to the side as she stopped in front of him.

"That's against the rules." He remained silent looking at the ground.

She paced again. "He was found with a dead girl and has been arrested."

George was pissed but he was too smart to fuck with her. Not yet anyway. The guards were ready to drop him at her command. This wasn't the time. He had to be patient.

He knew what she was capable of.

"I didn't mean for that to happen." He stated starring down at his feet.

She stopped in front of him.

"You didn't mean for it to happen." Her voice was quiet. Calculated.

She repeated matter of factly.

"No. Ma'am I didn't. I'm sorry" He stated in his best southern drawl, the one that drove all the ladies crazy.

"I didn't mean to offend you."

Not meaning a word of it, but still managing to sound sincere.

"I wanted to go to town, I had some needs, and I couldn't control them. I didn't want to go alone and when he begged me to let him come, I thought we would go have some harmless fun and I'd have him back here before the sun came up."

"Harmless fun..... HARMLESS FUN?? Her voice raised to a shrill frequency.

"You let him rip a prostitute limb from limb, and then left him alone, to get caught by the police, all because you had some needs. What needs do you have, that are so important?" George looked down at the floor. She waved one of the guards away.

"Well?"

"Female needs." He replied.

"Oh I see….You compromised my entire organization, so that you could get your little dick wet." George gritted his teeth. He hated her. He took a step towards her and heard the guard cock his gun.

He wanted to slap the shit out of her, but knew he was in no position to do so right now. He stepped back quickly.

His fear of her was long gone, replaced by hate, but he wasn't a stupid man.

He would bide his time. George chose his words carefully.

"I stopped at the payphone to call you. I couldn't get him to come off of the girl.

I wanted to dump her, but he freaked and wanted to keep her. He wouldn't get back in the van. He wouldn't listen to me, and I didn't want to hurt him, without your permission. Priestess I didn't mean for this to happen. I tried to get him back in the van. If I had stayed, we would both be in jail. I can fix this."

He lowered his eyes to the floor. He already knew by her body language that he had won her.

She sighed, stepping closer and looking directly into his eyes.

"Well how do you propose to do that?" she asked, as she sat down on the rod iron bench, patting the spot next to her for him to sit.

"I can get him out." George said as he moved into the place next to her.

"Pray for your sake that you do, and the next time you have female needs, you know where to come." Anita whispered, as she ran her hand up his thigh.

She waved him away, dismissing him once again.

He walked away, and as soon as he reached his room he punched the wall several times, releasing his anger.

He was done with this bitch and her stupid cult. He was better and smarter than her and he would make her pay for all the embarrassment. To add insult to injury she actually thought he would stoop to fucking her.

They would all pay.

Lupe and her grandmother spent a lot of time at the cabin with Megan and the Sam.

Tom, Grey and Mark continued their search. The composite sketch hadn't produced ant significant leads. The trail had gone dead.

The women prepared meals together, and kept each other company.

It was safer to be together. It gave Megan comfort too.

She waited for Seraphine to have another vision, but as Lupe informed her that they only came when they were meant to.

Megan was dying inside wondering, and worrying about her daughter.

They settled into a routine.

Grey helped her during the day, and Mark stayed up with the Sam at night.

For the most part he had started to rest through the night again.

Mark hadn't been sleeping much anyway, and was the insomniac of the house. He patrolled everything.

Night after night he watched his family sleep and walked the house worrying about his daughter and praying night after night that she was alive, and safe.

He thought back to all those months when he had searched for Megan and Grey trying to stifle the guilt. There had been no shred, that they were alive.

He couldn't stop it. Mark didn't know why he kept rehashing this scene.

It ran through his mind over and over, like a reel.

His feelings had been all over the place. They still were, and he hadn't felt the same since. A shadow loomed over him.

All he wanted was to find his daughter. He wished things were normal and he could provide a home for his family.

A normal home. Not this constant running.

This life was ok for him. He was used to running.

Mark had been running his entire life, from love, and from himself. Now here he was, not able to hide from this.

He had to stay and face it head on. Find his baby girl, and get it all back together. Knowing it wouldn't be over until the cult was disbanded and Anita was gone.

By gone he didn't mean jail time. Mark meant gone; dead.

He would kill her himself, if he got the chance.

Starring out of the window, he watched a lone coyote walked across the field.

"Hey" Greys voice said quietly behind him.

"Hey." Mark answered. He had not heard him walk up. Another problem, and something else to beat himself up about.

"Can't sleep?"

"You know, I'm just seeing what's going on."

Greys deep voice resonated.

"It's gonna be ok. We are going to find her and you will have your family back together. I can feel it."

"You old shit. You don't have any psychic ability." Mark chuckled.

"I'm not saying I do." He replied in a defensive tone.

"I'm not Seraphine, but all I'm saying is, if she wasn't alive I would know."

"Ok" Mark said, watching Grey get offended.

"Calm down old timer. I get it."

"I don't think you do," Grey replied.

"You are just killing time. How long we been sitting here? You're blaming yourself, wasting time. You need to get it together. We should be out searching. But you're too busy having a pity party, while we sit like ducks.

 It's not your fault. You did every single thing you could do. EVERITHING. There was nothing else you could have done, man,-nothing. Just like when my family died.

It was so far out of my hands. But I hid and blamed myself for years." The big man stuck his hands in his jeans pocket, dropping his head in shame.

"I holed myself up, in that fortress and didn't let anyone in. I blamed myself.....but in reality there was nothing I could have done."

Mark wanted to say something. Something shitty, just to make himself feel better, and to piss Grey off so he would go away. He didn't want to talk about it. But he knew he Grey was right.

He had been procrastinating. Checking the data files, making little day trips. Patrolling the house. He was too afraid to take his eyes off Megan and Sam; Afraid to leave the family that he had almost lost.

"You're right. I'm afraid to leave them." He admitted.

"What if something happens?"

He stood, and paced the floor.

"I can't leave them here alone. Last time, I WAS there, and she almost died. I was right there and they slipped through my fingers."

"Well we gotta figure something out. But you're right, this isn't a safe place. We have to put them somewhere ....maybe a safe house."

The moment the words came out of Greys mouth he hated them.

"Safe house? What a joke." Mark said.

"Your family went to a safe house and an hour later they were dead in the road." He remembered the blood and the snow mixing together, and the sight of Grey falling to his knees.

"I shouldn't have said that." Mark said apologetically.

"That was a line of shit. I'm sorry too." Grey said.

"Somewhere safe, I mean a place with someone we can trust. That little girl isn't safe either. SHE WAS THE ONE THAT GOT AWAY. You know the profile. He's coming back for her. Guys like that they don't like to lose."

"He may have gotten the other one, but she wasn't the target, Lupe was."

"I know I've been thinking that too. He will come for her."

"We have to find a place, or we have to bring them with us. And we need to bring the old lady too."

 He was referring to Seraphine.

"That old lady can cook." Grey said.

"Man is that all you think about.....food?"

"Well it's pretty high on my list. I don't have much else going for me."

"Ok then we have to figure something out. When is Tom going to be back?"

"I don't know, he said he had some things to check out."

"We need to get with him. The solstice is coming up, in a few months.

Seraphine said that she is alive. That makes me believe that she is waiting for the solstice. She is going to sacrifice my daughter. We can't let that happen"

"I know. I've been thinking about it to."

"If she hurts one hair on her head I will tear her limb from limb…"

"I know" Grey interrupted him.

"Save it for when we find her and that crazy Albino fucker. I'm going to kill him, with my bare hands, beat him down, till there's nothing left of him." Grey said.

"Damn freak of nature I don't know where she dug him up at."

Mark nodded in agreement.

"Your right we need to kill them both. That's the only way this thing is ever going to end. We can't go through the FBI. There can't be a trial or court. This has to end on our terms. We have to find out where Tom stands, if he stands with us, or with the law. Agreed?"

"Agreed," Grey answered, "I'm with you. You know that I don't care who I gotta kill. I'll kill everybody."

Of all things in the world, Mark knew this, as the truth. He had seen Grey in action, on more than one occasion.

When his family had been killed, they both knew the leak was CIA. He had seen Grey take down most of their headquarters, ripping the building to shreds and anyone that got in his way.

It took six men to take him down. In the end they let him go on his way, not to keep him quiet, but to save their own lives.

"Don't get excited." Mark said, you can leave some people alive. You know the innocent people, and the cook." He chuckled.

"Oh like the guy you stabbed in the hand?"

"He wasn't innocent. He was a snitch, a traitor. He has ties to the cult."

"He was CIA."

"That bastard turned." Mark said.

"Well you impaled his hands on the table."

"Technicality" he replied. I let him back up, and he had it coming."

"Yeah well, we'll see. You know they let him go."

"What? How the hell do you know that?"

"Tom told me."

" Why didn't you tell me?"

"You don't need to know everything, you just get pissed off." Grey stated.

"Then you act up."

"I act up?" Mark said, in annoyance.

"Yes." Grey said nodding his head.

Mark took a deep breath and rubbed his temples.

"Look dude, I need to know, what you know. We need to be on the same page.

I need to know everything. Don't keep things from me."

"I apologize, Just thought you'd flip out about it."

Grey pulled a red flannel shirt on over his white t –shirt, covering his massive arms.

"I didn't want you losing your head. I need you, to keep it together."

Mark shook his head in agreeance. He had been an asshole. He was caught up in the past. He was no good to anyone like this.

"I got this." He lied, slapping Grey on his shoulder.

"I hope so." He replied under his breath, as Mark walked into the house. It was still dark outside as he entered the bedroom. It was time to stop all this, he thought. Grey was right. He needed to get back to where he was before, and he knew the place he needed to make amends first.

He carefully pulled the blanket off Megan's sleeping form, and inched her panties down. He parted her legs and lifted her hips to his face. "Yes"…… this was a good place to start.

Tom came in at first light. Grey intercepted him at the door. He wanted to talk to him alone before Mark woke up.

He had been up drinking coffee and waiting.

"Hey." The big man said.

"What's up?"

"Not much another dead end." Tom poured himself a cup of coffee.

"Any other leads?"

"Nothing great, a few farm houses they are checking out today. No one is talking."

"Anything on the sketch?"

"No nothing." Tom said discouraged. He had been working so hard, trying to make things right. He was at a loss. The FBI was holding back, and he didn't understand why. He assumed it was about Mark and Grey being former CIA.

Or maybe they were involved. He couldn't be sure.

Everything was political, and since the Massive scandal, with numerous politicians exposed everyone was keeping quiet. He knew the bureau, and the CIA were tired of the cult, and would try to deal with them in their own way.

He knew they had to get to them first, if they were going to have any chance of finding the child.

"We need to talk." Grey said.

"Let's go outside." Tom followed him off the porch, onto the red clay drive.

The sun was coming up the air was damp and cold. That was the thing about the dessert.

It would get up to 110 in the day and down to 20 at night.

Grey's six foot eight frame crunched the ground beneath his feet.

Although Tom was tall, he had to take two steps to every one of Greys.

"What's up?"

"First of all I need to know where you stand."

"What do you mean?" Tom asked.

"This isn't going to end with prison time, or courts. There are too many people involved. When we get Josephine back, we have to end it in our own way. No FBI, or CIA, or police. You understand?"

Tom nodded.

"Yes. I'm with you."

"You sure? Because if you're not, we can part company, in friendship. No hard feelings." He was giving him an out if he wanted it.

"Hell no. I'm in." They shook hands.

"Besides I got a score to settle for almost getting my ear shot off."

"That was Mark wasn't it?" Grey asked.

Tom laughed. "Hell yeah, but I don't mean him."

They laughed for a moment. Grey was glad he decided to stay. They needed all the help they could get.

"Now, the next order of business," Grey said.

"I think we need to move them. It's not safe here. We have been here too long. I don't want them to be a target. Too much time has gone by.

Everyone is getting complacent. While we sit here holding our dicks, They are reorganizing." Tom knew he was right.

"It's dangerous."

"We were in that hotel room three days, and they found us. I'm not gonna be a sitting duck again. It's time to go."

"I think your right. I've been thinking about it too" Tom replied.

"Here's the other thing, Mark is so busy blaming himself. I love him like a brother but he's got too much invested, to have a clear head right now. All he can think about is that baby. Not that I blame him."

They continued to walk. Frost had settled during the night. Grey could see his breath.

"Right now his edge is gone. He can't get over his guilt. It's got him by the balls. He's wound so tight we have to watch him close."

"Should we just leave him with her and the baby?" Tom asked.

"I don't think we should leave him alone." Grey replied. He wasn't leaving anyone behind.

"He's not making a lot of sense." Tom said. "He called me last night, ranting about me, conspiring with the FBI and withholding information."

"I know what it is to feel that kind of guilt and I know here he's heading. I don't like it. It's a dark road. If he heads down it, he will be alone."

"If he loses his child he will flip the fuck out."

Grey knew this to be true. He had himself come from a loving home, and a large family. He had been loved, and had loved before he had his own family.

Mark on the other hand had not. He had always been a loner, and if he lost his family, he would not come back from it.

"Lupe isn't safe either, you know that psycho is coming back for her."

"I know that's the profile. Guys like him, can't stand to let one get away. Grey leaned on the fence and took a drink of his coffee.

"Where are you thinking?"

"I want to stay in Arizona. This is where they are. I can feel it in my bones this is where it will go down."

"We have to find a safe house."

"Dude," Grey said, "Don't ever use that word again. Especially around Mark. We don't say that one."

"Ok?" Tom inquired.

"It's a long story, but we have to find a place where no one can find them." He nodded his head.

"What about Red Bird?" Grey asked.

"What about him?"

"He's the head of the tribal council, and an elder. He knows this whole area, and has access to the entire reservation. Its protected land no one goes in or out without the approval of the council." Tom said.

"That's a great idea man."

The door fell open and Mark walked outside.

"I know you two old bastards aren't talking about me." He said. Grey turned toward him.

"As a matter of fact we were just talking about how ugly you are, and short."

Tom smiled.

"No, seriously, we were trying to think of a place to go." They filled him in on their idea.

"The Indian reservation?"

"It's a good idea, its protected land." Grey stated.

"Let's talk to Redbird about it." Tom added.

"Yeah, will they let people that aren't Indian in?"

"I don't know, that's why we have to talk to Redbird."

Grey smacked Mark in the back of the head.

"All right let's do it."

Grey called Redbird, and after a lengthy conversation, he agreed that it was a good idea. He was in fear for Lupe's life as well.

He would talk to the tribal council, and try to get their blessing.

Tom was the first to receive the call, that the Albino had been arrested, and that the man in the composite sketch was on the loose.

He put down his cell phone, "They picked up the Albino."

The two men sitting at the table starred at him.

"What happened?" Grey said.

"They found him sitting on the side of the road with a dead mangled prostitute.

They are holding him over in Silver falls. I'm going to head down there."

Grey and Mark looked at each other. This confirmed it. The albino and the serial killer together. The ties to the cult had just confirmed themselves.

"Go." Grey said. He knew Mark needed this.

"I'll watch the family."

Mark nodded. There was no one he trusted more. Redbird called just as they were getting ready to leave, to let them know that the tribal council had voted.

They felt as if the murders were too close to home, and would offer up any assistance and protection that they could, especially since it affected some of their own.

The reservation spanned hundreds of miles. Megan, Sam, and Redbird's family would be well hidden.

Mark took the receiver from Grey.

"Can you ensure my family's safety?" He asked.

"I will relocate your family myself, and I can promise you I will protect them with my life. My family will be there too."

"Where will you be taking them?" Mark asked with a heavy heart.

"The only stipulation of the council is that no one can know where we are going. They don't want this war brought on to the reservation."

"So I'm not going to know where my family is?" Mark smiled crazily, shaking his head. "I don't think so."

"You do what he says." Grey interjected.

Mark covered the receiver.

"What the hell are you talking about? He's saying that I'm not going to know, where my own family is going. Does that sound familiar?" He shouted.

They stood nose to nose. Tom stepped between them. He had seen them both in action, and didn't want it to turn ugly.

"That's a low shot." Grey said.

"I'll let it go because it's you. Don't step over that line again." He whispered to him.

Mark got back on the phone.

"Can you guarantee their safety?"

"I will. I can. My family will be there too. Lupe is the one that got away. Tom says the man will come back for her and possibly my whole family. I will be with them. The men I have chosen are rogues. They live far in the reservation and don't mingle with outsiders. There won't be any compromise there. I will stay with them, and go into hiding also. All I can tell you is, we will be deep in the reservation."

Mark looked at Grey as he paused. He held the phone and starred into Grey's eyes.

His heart was torn. They were asking him to trust strangers with his family.

Grey nodded his head. He sighed and starred at the floor, not wanting to make a mistake. Redbird waited patiently at the other end of the phone.

Grey grabbed his shoulder, and nodded again, when he looked up.

"All right then." Mark said, defeated.

"When will you be coming?"

"Tonight at sunset. It is better to travel in the dark. We know the way."

"Thanks man, I'll see you then." He hung up the phone and ran his hand through his hair.

"I know this is hard." Grey said.

"I got mixed feelings too. But I know what will happen if we stay here. We both do. This is the lesser of the two evils."

Mark told him when Redbird was coming. "Guess we'll go to Silver Falls after he picks them up. That Albino freak isn't going anywhere." Tom said.

Later that afternoon, Lupe and Seraphine, returned to the house with their backpacks.

Mark was in the room with Megan, trying to explain the situation, while Grey played with Sam in the kitchen. They beat wooden spoons on pots together, and drove everyone crazy.

"You want me to go to an Indian reservation? Alone, in the middle of nowhere? How am I supposed to find my daughter there?" She was angry and confused.

Mark took her face in his hands.

"I will find her. You have to trust me….. Look, I can't keep you safe here…. I can't. If you stay here I can't protect you."

"And what if it's too late?" She cried.

"I pray that it's not, but either way I will bring her home to you."

They looked at each other, and she trusted he would do whatever he had to do, to bring Josephine home. She wrapped her arms around him and clung to him.

"Are you going to come and see us?" she said, as the tears started.

"No. I won't know where you are. It's safer that way. If they get to me, they can do whatever they want, to me, and I won't know anything, except that you will be on the reservation.

It stretches for hundreds of miles. You will be protected. Redbird will make sure that you are safe. He's an honorable man. Seraphine and Lupe will be with you. they aren't safe either."

"When will this ever end?" Megan sobbed.

Mark took her into his arms and held her as she cried.

"I just want to have a normal life." She said with her face pressed to his chest.

"I know." He kissed her then, and like this morning, the passion that had lain dormant for so long had returned. He pulled her shirt over her head and unzipped her jeans. He kissed her face, her neck and across her belly.

His hand found that spot that made her moan with pleasure, but today it was mixed with tears.

He made love to her then, slowly, softly, cradling her face in his hands, and kissing her, until they were both exhausted. She lay with her head on his chest.

"You find our daughter, and bring her home."
"Yes ma'am I will." He had renewed hope, because she believed in him."

They showered together in silence, each lost in their own thoughts. When they dressed he was all business. It reminded her of when they had first arrived at the cabin. It pissed her off then. Now she understood it.

"Pack your things. Redbird will be here soon. Pack light." He told her after they dressed.

"I love you." Megan said. He walked out of the room with no response. She packed her things, and Sam's, with a heavy heart.

Mark headed straight out the door, off the porch and down the dirt road. He had to walk it off. His anxiety level was going through the roof. He didn't know if the anxiety he felt was genuine, or if he was overreacting because of the past.

If he was going to be effective, he had to turn it off. Passing Grey in the hallway, their eyes met. Grey starred at him. He didn't like the look in his eyes, but he understood it.

Redbird arrived at sunset as promised. He drove a dark brown van.

Seraphine and Lupe loaded their belongings into the back.

Tom said goodbye and headed into town for the night.

Grey kissed the baby and hugged Megan goodbye. He pushed a small pager into

her hand. "Push the red button if you get into trouble. It has a tracking device." He whispered.

"Thank you." she said slipping it in her pocket.

Just when she thought Mark was not going to say goodbye, he sprinted around the side of the house.

Mark rushed to lean into the van, and pulled her to him, holding her tightly. She could feel him shaking. He tried his best to control his breathing.

"I love you babe. You are everything to me. Be safe." He whispered. She could see his jaw clenching. Megan could tell he was close to tears.

"Love you." She said through her own tears. No other words would come.

He leaned in and kissed his son on the head.

"You make sure he always knows I love him." He said quietly. He shut the van door, and walked around to the driver's side. He looked at Redbird.

"Take care of them. If even a hair on her their heads gets kinked, I'm coming for you." He whispered eerily.

Redbird nodded his head. He tipped his hat to Grey, and pulled the van out of the drive. As soon as they were out of sight, Mark walked away and punched the post of the porch over and over, until his knuckles bled.

Grey said nothing, considering he felt like doing the same.

"We're staying out here till morning to make sure no one is following, and give them time to get where they are going." Grey said.

He set the M16 next to him, as he sat down in the porch chair. The wind would pick up during the night, covering the tracks of the tires. They alternated making coffee and pulled their jackets around them in the frigid night air.

Guns all around them, they sat there in silence, till first light. Mark deviated between wanting to cry, and wanting to kill. By first light, he had pushed it away, turned it inward.

Grey stood up and stretched.

"Rock and Roll son."

They loaded their bags into the back seat of the Jeep. Grey called Tom to tell him they were heading to Silver falls. He agreed to meet them there.

An hour later they pulled up at police station. Grey studied the small building.

It had too many windows and wasn't a safe location. This was a poor area and the building reflected it. Not much serious crime came through here. Your occasional drunk, and maybe a shop lifter.

The Indians ran all this, and had their own way of dealing with things.

Tom met them at the door and flashed his badge. They were led into a small interrogation room. They all looked the same. No matter where you went. Small sterile rooms.

A guard brought the Albino in. Shackled and handcuffed. Grey put his hand on Mark's arm as he felt him getting up.

"Easy man." He said quietly. He had been worried about him not taking action, now this was the other side of Mark, he had not seen in many years. A side that when unleashed was dangerous and hard to reel in.

"We need to ask him some questions."

The room was silent until Tom spoke.

"What's your name." He asked in his southern drawl.

No answer.

Finally the Albino looked up pink eyes boring onto Greys. Disturbing and freakish. He was still covered in scratches and dried blood.

"Francis." The albino stated.

"Do you know where Anita is?"

"I'm not supposed to talk to anyone."

"Do you know where she is?"

"At home. I don't drive. Only George drives the van." He sounded like a child.

Tom looked at Mark. He pulled out the composite sketch.

"Is this George?"

"Yes." Francis got excited. "He's my friend."

"What's his last name?"

"He is George Cane. He lives with the priestess at the house. He has his own room and gets to drive the van."

"This is getting nowhere." Mark said.

"He's a retard." Mark whispered to Grey in annoyance.

"You're not supposed to use that word." Grey replied.

"Your fucking shitting me right?" Mark asked.

"Just saying."

The Albino stared at him.

"I know YOU. You shot me. You hurt me. You shot me." he continued to yell. His voice rising and getting louder and louder. He was escalating. The guards came in and removed him. Tom and Mark agreed to wait in the car, while Grey met with the chief. He was a white man, which surprised Grey.

The deputy was Indian, as was almost everyone else in town. He explained to Chief Johnson that he had to be kept in protective custody. That he was an important part of a case, and not to let him out of his sight.

He reiterated that security was of the utmost importance.

The chief promised he would have him moved to Johnson county, and tack on some charges, just in case.

He was a short, bald fellow, with beady brown eyes, and a beer belly.

Chief J., as his men called him, explained that when he was being arrested he hung on to the dead prostitute not wanting to give her up, screaming that she belonged to him.

They literally had to pry him off of her corpse.

When Grey came out he told them what the Chief had said. Hopefully it would buy them some time and another chance to talk to the Albino, or Francis as he now called himself.

Inside sheriff Johnson propped his feet on his desk.

"That stupid ass," he said to his deputy, as soon as Grey walked out.

"All those FBI guys are the same. They think they run shit. This is my county, and I don't answer to the fucking FBI. That Freak is staying right here, till I decide what to do with him."

They laughed and slapped each other on the shoulder. "Let's go to lunch."

Tom Ran George Crane through the FBI data base. There was not much of a history. He was your average white guy, in the rat race. He had all the makings of a serial killer, abandoned by his parents, fired from his job, losing his life savings, and turning to speed.

His last know location was a drug rehab in Fester, Texas. From here he had disappeared.

It was Tom's guess that he had hooked up with the cult then, almost a year and a half ago, and also the time when the murders started.

He was sure he was their guy, and the Albino had confirmed his tie to the cult.

At first light Redbird pulled the van into the small clearing. He got out and whistled three times. Several Apache braves appeared on the horizon.

They stopped and helped Redbird load the bags onto the pack mule that followed on a lead. Redbird helped Megan onto her horse, a palomino. She was tame and good natured. Redbird had chosen her specifically for Megan.

He handed Sam to her, and a large scarf to tie around him to secure his body to hers. He slept through the process.

Lupe and Seraphine also mounted their horses. Everyone was quiet. They all knew what was at stake.

Megan thought of Mark and the others and hoped they were safe. She knew Grey would keep him safe. She trusted him.

She had a feeling this was the beginning of a long journey. She pulled her son closer to her with one hand, and hugged him, as the horses began to walk in a line.

Lupe and Seraphine made small talk.

"Where are we going?" Lupe asked.

"Hush child." Redbird said "Enjoy the ride."

They rode most of the day. Even when Sam was awake he watched the scenery go by. He was unusually quiet, as if he also knew they were heading on a long journey. Long after dark they came to a small oasis.

There were braves there already. It made her uneasy that they had machine guns. Most of them were dressed in only jeans or tribal clothing.

Redbird led her to a white tipi. It was much larger than it appeared. It was clean and a fire burned in the middle, the smoke traveling up to an opening in the top. There were fur pelts on the ground. Megan took off her shoes and put Sam down on the thick furs that were made into a makeshift bed for her.

Sam watched her pull off her thick coat and sweater. Lupe poked her head into the flap and handed Megan a bowl. My uncle said to give you this she said.

"What is it?" It smelled good. It is elk and vegetables. He says to eat it all. He also sent this." She handed her a small bag.

It was a flask with goat milk and mashed vegetables for Sam who was eating solid foods. He babbled as he crawled around, feeling the furs with his chubby little fingers.

Megan fed and changed him. He lay drinking his sippy cup, with goat milk, as she ate her bowl of food. It was good. She was hungry, and quickly devoured it.

Lupe told her of a spring and went to get her some water.

She was glad for her help. Laying back she pulled Sam close to her. He was all she had of Mark now.

The furs were comfortable and she started to doze.

She felt safer here than she did at the cabin. Lupe came back in, with the water.

"Boy that's cold." Megan said, taking a drink.

"Yes, the whole spring is like that."

"My grandma says that I should help you with the baby and everything you need."

"Well thank you. I appreciate that. I'm sorry you were dragged into all this."
"It's not your fault." Lupe said.

"The people after us are from a cult and my mother is their leader. She stole my daughter and wants to kill her, and all of us, so it kind of Is."

"I didn't know." Lupe said. "It still isn't your fault."

"My mother died when I was a baby, and Seraphine raised me."

"She is a good woman." Said Megan.

"Yes but very strict." Lupe laughed.

"Well I think we will be safe here for a while."

"My grandma says I must hide here with you so the dark man doesn't come and kill me."

It hurt her heart, to hear an innocent girl talk so frankly about it.

"Hopefully Mark, Grey and Tom will have this all figured out soon so we can all go home."

"I hope so too." Lupe replied. She missed her friends, and even the club.

"I think it will be fun. Can I stay the night with you and the baby, one night?"

"Sure but not tonight ok? I just want to get settled in and get my thoughts together."

"Ok soon then." Megan shook her head in agreement.

"Lupe hesitated in the doorway. I just feel bad about something that Seraphine said to Grey.

"What did she say?" Megan asked.

"I'm not supposed to tell."

"She had a vision?" Lupe nodded her head.

"Yes, my Grandma told Grey that one of them will die, and only two of them would return." Megan's heart skipped a beat.

"When did she tell him that?"

"This morning, while he was helping us load the van."

"Oh my god." Megan said, dreading the thought of it. What Grey must be going through, knowing one of them wouldn't make it. She didn't understand what the purpose of telling him would be, except to put him on edge.

"Thank you for telling me Lupe, if she tells you anything else you have to let me know." Megan held on to Lupe's hand, looking her in the eyes.

"I will I promise." She whispered, leaving the tipi.

Megan lay back down, and once again pulled Sam to her, but this time it gave her little comfort.

She wondered which one of them it would be, and felt guilty for praying that it wouldn't be Mark. But she couldn't help it.

He was the love of her life, and the father of her children. She prayed for Grey too. She had grown to love him deeply.

As they drove Grey thought about what Seraphine had said. That one of them would not be coming back. He believed in her visions. So far they had all come true.

It was eerie how she was able to see things. He would not tell Mark. It would only fuck up his mind and trip him up.

He figured it would be him anyway. It had to be. He was the only one with nothing to lose.

Grey had lived his life, and he longed to be with his wife and daughter again. He knew Mark had Megan and the babies, and they needed to have a normal life. Tom had his whole life ahead of him.

It was ok with him. He was ready to give up the ghost, As soon as he knew they were all safe.

If there was a god in heaven, he would be the one.

Much later that afternoon Tom headed into Albuquerque for an FBI meeting.

Mark and Grey decided to check out some of the houses that Tom had crossed off the list, dismissing them for one reason or another, without really looking at them.

Grey thought this to be a careless thing, and a serious underestimation on his part. He wasn't as thorough as he should be.

Everything wasn't always cut and dry. Sometimes people were so fucked up, they deviated, their behavior. That's what Grey despised about the FBI, they were quick to lay down judgement, and based everything on a profile. There was no color, only black and white. Everything was in a neat little box. If it didn't fit they didn't want to even give it a second look.

They drove from house to house. The first five hadn't panned out. The last house was on a long gravel drive. There was no way to go in without being seen.

They pulled into a thickly wooded area, outside the 6 foot stone wall to the north.

The wall had barb wire over it. It was an unusual sight for this area, considering there were mainly rural farms, and the reservation to the west.

Grey pulled himself up to take a look over the wall. There were metal shutters on every window, and outside the front door stood an armed guard.

Grey scanned the back for a marijuana crop, but didn't see anything illegal growing.

That only left one thing. It had to be the place. Tom had missed it. Later as they surveyed the perimeter, a limousine pulled up and honked the horn. Grey was hanging on the wall watching. The door opened and a woman came out.

Grey recognized her from her picture. He dropped down, quietly without a sound.

"Holy fuck. It's her." He whispered.

"Who?" mark asked, knowing in his gut of whom he spoke.

"Anita."

Mark felt his senses reeling. "WHAT? Are you sure? Let me see." He hoisted himself up, where he could get a visual.

"Holy shit......" he whispered, dropping back down.

He stood, running his hand through his hair. He had to think. Grey leaned into the car. He pulled his 9mm and cocked it.

"Let's go. I'm gonna kill that bitch." Grey whispered in an ominous tone.

This time it was Mark that interceded. Suddenly it was clear. This was not the time to overreact.

"No. We have to wait." He said sternly.

"Wait? for what?" the big man replied.

"We don't know if the baby is even in there. She may have her somewhere else. We aren't doing a thing till we know for sure. If you kill Anita now, we may never find out where she is."

Grey dropped his head, and his weapon.

"Your right." He pulled himself up next to Mark.

"I just really want to kill her." He sighed.

They watched Anita get into the back seat of the limo. It pulled out of the gravel drive. After waiting a few moments, they followed.

Mark pulled his hat down over his face staying a safe distance behind.

The Limo pulled off, onto an exit. They steered in behind them. Farmland stretched for miles. They had not been spotted.

The car pulled into a field as they passed by. Mark pulled into a wooded area far enough where the Jeep couldn't be seen from the road.

The two men ran through the trees to the edge of the clearing. Grey was already down on his stomach looking through the binoculars.

"What's happening?" Mark asked.

"The one guy got out of the car. He's a big fat guy with a Stetson and a suit.

They are shaking hands. He's handed her a briefcase. She's opening it. I can't see what's inside. Now she is handing him an envelope. Here comes another car, Ok another dude is getting out. He's in a suit and hat too" Grey reported.

"Can you see the plates? Yep, they are both Texas. BHI 896. I can't make out the other one, he's parked at too much of an angle, but it looks like Texas too."

"They look like rich dudes." Grey whispered. "I think I've seen the fat one on TV."

"She must be banding up with them." Mark responded.

They shook hands and the two cars, with the men, pulled away.

Anita stood there for a moment longer, talking on her cell phone. Then she got into the backseat and her car drove away.

Mark and Grey stayed put. They knew where the house was. They agreed to wait till dark.

"Let's go get some food and then well honker down. Watch the place for a few days maybe a week, see what we can see." Grey said, rubbing his belly.

"I'm hungry."

Mark shook his head. He was always hungry.

"I thought that when you got old your appetite slowed down" he teased.

"I'm only 36." Grey said in annoyance.

Mark didn't want to wait either but he knew it was the smart thing to do. Maybe this was why the FBI was holding off, if Grey had seen one of the men on TV, it was probably some politician.

They stocked up on coffee, chips, and sandwiches. Parking back in the thicket where they could see the driveway, and scale the wall if need be.

Mark climbed the wall again. He hoped there wasn't a dog. He knew there was no surveillance camera. That had been checked that out earlier, with the binoculars.

The Guard was back in place and as far as he knew Anita was back in the house. The dark blue Sedan parked in the driveway. Mark would have to find a way inside. They talked and reminisced the rest of the night. It was like old times.

They both wondered why they hadn't heard back from Tom. His meetings must have gone longer than expected.

Mark was getting suspicious, but he kept it to himself.

Megan and Lupe spent most of their days together. They gathered water, picked vegetables, and helped in the Garden. Sam had started walking, almost overnight. On a daily basis, he gave her a run for her money, and after lunch, he got into an ant mound.

Seraphine mixed up a concoction of herbs to soothe the bites.

Sam the hippie, was also a notorious dirt eater. She took her fingers to dig dirt out of his mouth on more than one occasion. He kept her on her toes. Now that he was mobile he was unstoppable.

The best thing was that he made her laugh, despite what they were going through. He was always up to something, and it made the days go by.

Lately, he slept through the night. Lupe helped her a lot, and Sam loved it when she played with him. She made him giggle and chuckle. He was a happy child and when he was amused he would roll on the ground holding his little belly and laughing.

Redbird had assigned a brave to Megan. He followed her everywhere.

His name was Mangas Coloradas, meaning Red sleeve. Megan found this name amusing, and as much as he annoyed her she referred to him as simply "The Sleeve."

He camped outside her Tipi at night, and as much as he annoyed her, it gave her a sense of safety. Two weeks had gone by and they were slowly settling in.

At dinner Seraphine had another vision. Megan was there, so she couldn't keep it to herself. She said the dark man was searching for them, the dark man and the white giant together.

She didn't know who to trust.

Megan believed that Redbird was a good man, and that he had good intentions, after all his family was here too. He was an Indian like most of the men here, yet somehow he made her uneasy.

The men mainly lived off the land, and some had never been off of the reservation. They had what they needed to sustain them.

Most were desert rats, so to speak. They had never left the reservation. Some of them, had never seen a white woman.

They starred at Sam. His long blond curls were a fascination to them. The men averted their eyes from Megan.

Strict instructions had been given to them, not to make eye contact.

A direct order from Redbird. They still looked when they didn't think anyone was watching.

Lupe thought of Raven often and prayed that she was safe and alive.

She hoped she would get the opportunity to see her again someday.

She felt guilty for running. Nightly she kept Raven in her prayers.

The days passed, and "The sleeve" taught Megan and Lupe how to plant a garden.

The braves had a large garden, but Megan wanted her own. It made her feel more self -sufficient.

The weeks passed. Megan's skin tanned easily, and it wasn't unusual for her hair to be in braids. She was starting to blend in.

Sam received his first bow and arrow, and he toddled along making it work.

Marks phone rang.

"It's Tom."

"Hey, what are you guys up to?" he asked.

"Nothing much," Mark replied as he looked over at Grey.

"We are looking at a few places but nothings panned out. Where are you?"

Grey's eyebrows lifted in surprise. Wondering why he was lying.

"I got some bad news," Tom said.

Marks heart sank.

"What?" He put the phone on speaker so Grey could hear.

"I just got a call from Silver Falls."

It seems Sheriff Johnson and his deputy are dead. You're Albino, Gone.

The place was torn to shreds.

Johnson, was almost decapitated, and the deputy's bowels were torn out and

wrapped around his neck."

"Someone busted him out then," Mark said. 'He couldn't have done all that on his
own."

"Are you guys going down there?"

"No, not if he's gone." Grey said.

"He'll turn up eventually. I told him to move that Crazy bastard."

Grey shook his head in disgust.

"Apparently he didn't listen." Mark said.

"Word on the street is, he was running his mouth over at the diner that he didn't like the FBI, and that he wasn't taking any orders from the "Mother fuckers."

Tom stated. "It was his jurisdiction."

"He ain't talking shit now." Grey mumbled.

"They've teamed up. I think it's the guy from the poster. He is crazy as hell."

"Where you fella's heading now?" Tom asked.

"We're out on route 80. Just wrapping it up. Gonna head back to the cabin and look again, Tomorrow."

Grey starred at him and smiled.

"We'll keep me posted."

Mark said goodbye and hung up the phone.

"Why you lying to him?"

"I don't know, something in his voice doesn't sound right."

"Man, he's our friend. He's been with us."

"I know, but there's just something."

He couldn't put his finger on it, but his gut was talking.

"When you talk to him face to face, you'll see that you're full of shit."

Grey joked, hoping he was right. Mark had the instincts of a lion, he could smell a rat from a mile away.

Grey hoped he was wrong. He knew Marks keen sense though. It was a worry.

"He is our friend."

"That's what you said about Carl."

"He was a kid."

"He was a damn snitch, and I'm not sure he wasn't tied to the cult in some way too."

"Jesus Christ, are we back to this shit?"

"Here we go again, we've been over this." Grey groaned.

He shook his head. It wasn't even worth the fight. Mark would go off on a rampage.

He didn't blame him. He knew that his emotions were still raw from almost losing his whole family.

Maybe he was right. Maybe the kid was a snitch.

Somebody was.

"What do you want to do? You really want to go back to the cabin?"

"Hell no. I'm sitting here till I figure out a way to get inside. I'm not leaving."

"OK I'll get some shut eye Grey said. Wake me up if you get tired.

I don't want that crazy bitch, or anyone else, creeping up on us out here."

He reclined his seat and closed his eyes.

Mark starred off into the night. He thought of Megan and the way her skin felt under his hands the last time they made love. He loved that woman. He loved her like he had never loved anyone. More than he loved himself. That wasn't much these days.

Mark hoped everything would go as planned, and he would see them again.

The albino and George rode in silence. As they drove, the cabin came into view.

"That's it." George said. He looked down at the paper he had scribbled the directions on.

"Let's see what we got." He said lightly. It was something his mother used to say.

"What are we going to do?" Francis asked.

"Were going to go in here and see about little Miss Megan, and that baby."

He had strict instructions not to kill the baby, or Megan. Anita wanted to do that herself. She would kill the baby and make her watch. Make her suffer as she had.

Then she would decide what to do with Megan. Anita had not told George but there had recently been some speculation among the elders in the church, who questioned the legality of using the baby for the Ascension.

Although she was part of the bloodline they weren't sure if it was a real bloodline, like that of Megan's direct one. Anita had therefore asked George to bring her alive.

She might still need her after all. "Hopefully her guard will be here too." George thought to himself.

"I'm going to show him what a real man is." Anita had said not to kill her. She didn't specify about anything else. The man could watch. It would fill George with pleasure.

Pulling out a serrated knife, a smile crept across his face. He carried a gun but this beautiful knife, was his drug of choice.

"I'll go around back." He whispered to Francis as they got closer.

"You wait here by the door in case anyone tries to escape." The albino nodded.

George looked in the windows. It was hard to see in the dark. There was a light on in the small hallway. A bed came into view that looked like it hadn't been slept in.

There were more bedrooms, that-didn't mean anything. It was after one am. Everyone was probably asleep, not expecting him. He smiled as he reached for the knob of the back door.

A crash startled him and made him jerk his hand back.

"Motherfucker." He cursed aloud realizing that Francis had kicked the front door in. He ran around, to the far side of the house.

"Christ Francis I don't know why she sends your ass with me, you can't get your shit together. If anyone's here, they know about us now."

He pulled his gun, and crept back around the back. There was no sound. Slowly he inched his way into the cabin, moving silently from room to room. There was nothing.

"Fucker's," he spat. "They are gone."

He walked back to the car and picked up his cell phone. Dialing the last number that had called him.

"They are gone. Where are they?" He listened intently to the voice on the other end. He hung up, and dialed Anita.

"We're at the cabin. They're long gone. Apparently they went into the dessert, with the Indians."

"Into the dessert?" She yelled. "Who the hell goes into the dessert? How are they going to survive out there? Are you sure this is reliable information?"

"Yes. That's what my source says."

"You better find them." She screamed into the phone. "I NEED HER."

"I can't drive through the damn dessert, You're gonna have to wait till they come out. This road ends in about 20 miles then there's nothing but sand."

"I suggest you drive down there and see what you can see." She said, as she slammed the phone in his ear. She screamed and beat the phone on the counter.

She had often wondered how her organization, her church had gotten as far as they had with these morons working for her.

"Alright." He said and hung up the phone. He didn't want Francis to know he wasn't in control.

He hated the heat and dirt and the sand. Worse than that, George hated hanging out with Francis. Who was a liability.

"Get in." he ordered, slamming his own door. He peeled out leaving a cloud of dust.

"Where we going George?"

"Jesus Christ," he thought to himself," he acts like he's my best friend. Fucking idiot."

He pulled over at the spot where the road ended. There was nowhere else to go. George got out and looked around. His Van would never make it through the thick sand. Not to mention that he had no idea which way they went. There were no tracks, no clues.

Pulling out his cell phone to call Anita, George realized there was no signal. He threw the phone onto the seat, and got back into the van.

Turning the vehicle around he squealed the tires for a hundred feet or more. Francis clapped and squealed. "Jesus" he muttered.

George was going to ditch him as soon as he got back to the house, shower, and go kill the old lady along with that bitch Lupe, that had gotten away.

He had wasted so much time watching her. George wasn't planning on letting her escape a second time. After they were all dead he would find Anita and fuck her up real good before he killed her.

Then Raven would be his. George wasn't really into rape, but he had been watching her for so long, he started to dream about the way her skin rippled when she moved.

It drove him crazy, and the fact that Anita had forbidden it, made it even more alluring. He was done with her.

She had convinced him that the cult, her church had been the thing for him, and it had pulled him out of his depression and his pill addiction for a while. Now he was tired of it. It was bullshit and he wouldn't be ordered around by that bitch.

It was all a joke. She thought she could control him and tell him what to do. No one ran him. George was his own man.

The sun was finally going down. It had been beating down on the van all day. His clothes stuck to his skin. When he dropped the freak off, he would shower, then he would go to work on the ladies.

He pulled the van into the driveway. As George exited, Mark was already on the wall watching with the binoculars.

"The gangs all here", he said quietly to himself.

George walked around the van and ripped the passenger door open. "Get the fuck out." He commanded.

The Albino got out of the passenger seat.

"Why George what did I do?"

"Just get out." He screamed.

The guard had already called for backup. They didn't screw around with George, especially when he was in a rage.

Grey joined Mark, just as Anita came out of the house. She looked around, and stepped outside.

"What the hell are you screaming about?"

"I'm bringing back your Fuck boy. He's a liability. He doesn't listen. He tore the fucking door off the house while I was trying to see if anyone was inside. I'm not going to Fucking babysit him." His voice was getting louder and louder.

Another guard came out. Anita instructed him to take Francis into the house.

She turned back to George.

"Lower your voice." Her words were ice.

"What did you find out?"

"The road ends, there's no one. Just desert."

"Maybe your informant was mistaken."

"No." he replied.

Mark and Grey looked at each other.

George rubbed his face. He itched all over. All he could think about was taking a shower.

"I'm going to take a shower. Then I'll go back out. BY MYSELF. I am going to take care of the other situation. I'm not going into the fucking desert. No one can survive in there."

He stormed past Anita and she waved him through the guards. She couldn't deal with him when he acted like this. She followed him into the house.

Mark dropped off the wall. Grey followed.

"He knows."

"How?"

"You tell me." Mark said.

"All he knows is they went into the dessert."

"It's been two weeks. No one else knows. How did he find out."

Mark was furious. It seemed like the long arm of the cult reached everywhere they turned.

"I don't know, Tom? One of the Indians? Someone close." Grey answered.

"Something is different about him."

"Maybe it's not him," Grey said. " Don't keep all your eggs in one basket. It could be someone else. We could set him up and find out."

"True, but I did tell him that we were going back to the cabin tonight."

They pulled out and parked further down the highway, waiting for George.

The two men watched him pull onto the highway. Mark eased the truck out behind him at a safe distance.

George pulled off the road right past Lupe's house, and cut off his lights. Mark passed him by and kept going.

Grey watched with the binoculars.

"We know he ain't gonna find anything, they are long gone. You wanna go back to the house?"

"Yeah"

"Tom knew that they were gone." Grey said.

Mark gave him a knowing look.

"Just an observation." Grey stated.

They headed back and pulled back into the wooded area. Mark scaled the wall for a third time.

"She doesn't have a lot of guards. They aren't expecting us."

"I'll watch the car," Grey said. "You see if there's a way in."

Once he dropped to the ground Mark hoped there weren't any dogs. Although he had been watching, you never knew.

He crept along the stone wall, on the inside this time. Mark made his way around back. Staying in the shadows.

There was no guard, only a shed in the back, and a light on in the kitchen.

He didn't want to go in without Grey, and compromise anyone's life.

He knew he still had time before the summer solstice, and if she was still alive she would be until then. Now time was of the essence with George knowing that Megan and Lupe were in the desert. Things needed to move along now.

Now he crawled on his stomach.

He saw the Albino cross the kitchen with a guard behind him. They went down a set of steps. There had to be a basement. At least two guards in the house, the Albino and Anita.

He saw no cameras. He never understood why there was not more security.

She really considered herself untouchable. He climbed back over the wall. Dropping into the darkness, Cutting his arm on the barb wire and wiping the blood on his shirt.

Grey waited for news. Mark filled him in.

"What do you want to do?"

"Stay put. We need to be still and wait."

Mark knew that was good advice and that he could trust Grey with his life. Although he hadn't made the best decisions lately he wasn't thinking like a hot head now. Although things had changed, he was being careful and would see it through till the end. They both would.

Marks phone rang. It was Tom. They exchanged glances. He answered and put it on speaker.

"I've been wired, get out of the cabin." The phone went dead.

Tom packed his bag quickly. He knew there was a breach at the bureau. He didn't know who. He hoped everyone was safe.

His parents had been relocated, taken to a safe house. He had to disappear. There wasn't much time.

Someone close to him was leaking secrets to the cult and to a serial killer. It made him sick to his stomach.

His whole life had been dedicated to the bureau. He lived and breathed FBI. He loaded his bag into the trunk of his rent a car, when the first shot rang out.

He ducked behind the car, cocking his weapon. He fired back, taking out the first shooter. He wasn't so lucky with the second one. He took a shot in the right lower abdomen. He fired back and wounded the second man.

Tom reached him, while he was still alive.

"Who sent you?" He groaned, leaning over the bleeding man.

There was no answer.

He pulled out his 9mm and put it to the man's temple.

"Who sent you?"

"CIA, They don't want you to expose the cult. They want it handled quietly. Because of a senator from Texas, and his brother."

Tom stood up, holding his side. He thought about shooting him anyway, but the man was bleeding out. It wouldn't be long now. He stumbled to the car, and drove away.

Megan started to look like an Indian. It had been several weeks. She was tan and looked healthy from all the sun, and healthy eating, from the garden and the hunt.

She had learned how to grow food.

Long braids hung past her shoulders.

At night they sat by the fire and told stories. She started to understand their language a little better, although she didn't let on.

They sang and danced. It was a quiet time in her life. Although she longed for her daughter and Mark, Her son was safe, and Megan felt like she could breathe.

The men had been together for a long time, and lived in simple harmony, as a tribe. Most of them had never set foot off the reservation and lived off the land their entire lives.

She learned more about the Apache and their ways. They were Kiowa Apache, and were native to Arizona and New Mexico.

The men looked fierce and strong. At night over the fire they told stories of Cochise Geronimo and Victorio, their most famous war chiefs.

They were Nomads, hunter gatherers. Redbird told her the word Apache meant "Enemy."

They hunted rabbit and took from the herd of goats, and wild turkey that they raised for food. They had all they needed.

Here she felt safe. She watched her son sitting in the sun, playing. She prayed for Josephine, Mark, Grey and Tom every day. She had asked Seraphine if he was still alive.

She did not see him in harm's way, although her visions of the dark man, was coming more frequently. The dark man's vision was clouded, so for now they were safe.

The dark man had been to the house and the cabin.

It was only a matter of time. One of them was injured, but Seraphine could not see which one. She kept it to herself. Megan needed some peace in her life.

The daily chores continued. It made the hours go by.

As of late another vision had plagued Seraphine. One of which she didn't dare speak of. She had to be sure.

Mark and Grey started to look like two mountain men. Beards growing, and Mark's hair had grown out. Grey had laughed saying they looked like old retired stoners.

Day after day they watched, knowing an opportunity would arise. Tom had dropped completely out of site. They had called the FBI and were told he was on vacation.

They didn't know what was going, on or where to look. They had to find the child and shut this cult down.

Mark wondered about his baby girl, things he had missed that he would never get back. Now he was missing time with his son, although he knew it was for a good cause.

For weeks they watched Anita come and go. She would meet up with people that came to the house on a weekly basis. There was no doubt she was trying to re-strengthen the cult. Her church as she called it.

They saw George come and go on a regular basis which told them that for now Megan and Sam were safe. Grey finally told Mark about the pager and the panic button, and right now he was glad for it.

Mark didn't understand why she didn't put much stock in her protection. When he had discussed it with Grey, he was under the impression that she was so full of herself that she never gave them a second thought. Anita was possibly looking for them, and they were right under her nose watching.

It was ironic, but Grey had seen her type before.

Mark on the other hand spent his days dwelling on past mistakes and wasted time, he would be grateful beyond belief, if he could just get his family back together.

Grey played solitaire on the dashboard of the truck. At night Mark climbed the wall and watched the yard.

Tonight was no different. He was looking into the back glass door, when Anita came around the corner.

He backed up quickly, sure that she had not seen him.

She was followed by a young woman.

It was Raven. He recognized her from her composite photo that the police and the FBI had distributed.

They sat down at the kitchen table. Anita smiled crookedly. Raven looked nervous.

He could see her hands clenching under the table. He couldn't make out what Anita was Saying, just a muffled voice through the glass. He wondered if she was a prisoner. He was sure it had at least, started out that way.

Anita and Raven stood and walked toward the hallway. Mark stood up and leaned in closer to see where they were going. Just as he leaned in, Raven turned and saw him. Their eyes met and locked, for a moment.

He froze in place. He had to think fast.

Mark put his finger to his lips to silence her. She in turn put her finger to her lips, and turned to follow Anita.

He prayed she would not give him away. Not sure what to make of the whole thing, Raven had never been seen exiting the house. She had to be a prisoner.

He backed into the shadows of the yard, and returned to the car to tell Grey.

"I hope she doesn't give you up." Grey said, shaking his head.

"That was stupid. We could lose everything we've worked for."

Mark knew how cut and dry Grey could get, but Grey was right. He knew he should have hung back and been more careful.

At least they knew Raven was alive. It was a start.

"I don't think she will." Mark replied.

They spent the rest of the night watching, and waiting. They next morning they were already on the wall, when the dark sedan pulled up.

The front door opened and Raven came out, and was ushered into the back of the car, by one of the guards, who entered the car behind her.

Mark jumped into the running truck and they followed.

They stopped in front of a clothing shop in town, and Raven got out alone.

Mark watched her enter the store. He had Grey pull around the block.

He walked down the sidewalk like he was window shopping and entered the store. He spotted her immediately.

Mark looked thought the racks, as if he was shopping, moving his way closer to the young woman.

She spotted him. He stood next to her watching the door.

"Are you Raven?"

"Yes." She replied hopefully. Someone was looking for her. It made her breathe a sigh of relief.

"Don't look at me." Mark replied. "Keep looking at the clothes. If he comes in and asks you about me, just say I was shopping for my wife and asked your opinion."

"Ok" she said quietly. He heart was pounding. Maybe he was here to save them.

"I'm Mark Westbrook. I am working with the FBI, he lied. He knew this would give him more credibility, and he didn't have the time to tell her everything, nor did he want to.

"The people you are living with are a cult. It's a very large organization, and they are not nice people. I don't have time to go into it all of it now, but you are in danger."

He was trying to be calm and not ask too much at once.

"Are you a prisoner?"

"Yes," Raven said. "The guy took me, and tried to kill me and my friend.

Lupe ran, and he pulled me into the van. I thought he was going to kill me, but he didn't. Then when I woke up, I was at the house. I am not allowed to leave unless Anita says so. She runs everything. It's her church. I think she is crazy."

"Are you ok? Did they hurt you?" Mark whispered.

"No, but they are going to kill me and Josephine too. We have to get out of there." She replied. "I can't leave. They lock me in."

"Josephine? You've seen her?" He stared at her. Marks heart skipped a beat, his pulse racing.

"I take care of her. We are locked in every night."

Mark wanted to drop to his knees.

"How is she? Is she healthy? Have they hurt her in any way?"

"NO, she's fine..." Raven replied, Staring at him. "I protect her. She is ....special in some way. They want to sacrifice her for some devil shit. You have to help us." She whispered desperately.

"She's my daughter." He said, not sure if it was the right thing to say, but he was unable to stop himself. It was a relief to be able to say it to another person.

Somehow it made it real. He hadn't been there like Megan to feel, and see her being born. He had had a hard time imagining her face, yet he loved her all the same.

Raven stared at him in disbelief.

"I need you to listen. Can you get out with her?"

"I don't know. I can try. They keep us way down in the basement." She whispered frantically.

"We've been watching the house every night. Tonight we can come in and get you, and Josephine. I didn't know if she was in there, for sure."

"NO." Raven said. She heard the old man's voice in her head, clear as day.

"It's too dangerous. You can't risk it. They will shoot at you, and a stray bullet will hit Josephine. "She is too important. I have been sent to be her protector. I have to be the one to bring her out."

Mark didn't understand how Raven knew these things, but he believed her. The look in her eyes said it all.

He nodded.

"We will be right there, if you can get out. If you're not out in the next two days Grey and I are coming in, so keep your head down, how many guards are in the house?"
"One guard at our door, one at the top of the stairs, and the guard outside."

"Who else is in the house?"

"Anita, and George, and the freaky Albino guy, I heard the guards talking. They have him locked in a cage."

"Try to get on the guards good side. Try to get out. We will be waiting. Don't take any chances though, only if you can get out safely." Raven watched Mitch exit the car and head toward the store.

"I have to go he's coming." Her urgent voice said.

"Be safe." Mark whispered, giving her shoulder a warm squeeze, as he walked away along the aisles.

The guard entered the store and saw Raven walking toward the register. He looked around just as Mark headed out the door. He nodded at him on the way out, and the guard nodded back.

Mitch waited, for Raven, and watched her climb into the car. He smiled to himself as he shut the door behind her. He and Greg had already discussed what they would do to this one, and that little girl, if given the chance. Anita had hired him despite his charges. He liked children, the younger the better.

Mark ran down the sidewalk, into the alley, where Grey waited with the truck.

Grey starred at Mark. His face was flushed and he could hardly speak.

"She's alive, my baby girl is alive."

After all this time, Mark finally lost it. The strength went out of his legs as he got into the passenger seat, put his hands over his face and cried. They were tears mixed with sorrow and joy.

A few minutes later, wiping his eyes, he spoke. He told Grey of the plan for her to get the baby out in the next two days.

"She is alive and healthy. They are locked in the basement. Raven is her nanny or babysitter, or whatever you want to call her. There are three guards in the house, plus Anita, George and the Albino. He's there somewhere, locked in a cage."

"Oh just them, I'm sure we can handle it. As a matter of fact ill just play cards and you take care of it."

"Are you being sarcastic?" Mark asked, puzzled by his sarcasm.

"No I just don't like it. You're putting it all on this girl, who doesn't know shit from Shinola. It will be a fucking miracle if she gets out, and if she doesn't that leaves the two of us, and all the psychos."

"I know, but it's a good plan. She thinks she can do it. She is part of this whole thing somehow. She said she was sent back to protect Josephine.

I don't know from where, but I believe her. Man it was a little eerie, and I don't understand it. This is bigger than us." Mark whispered as he ran his hand through his hair.

"I'm just not ready for anyone to die today. Especially you, or the baby, and not that girl either. I don't want that on my head."

Grey said slamming his hands down on the steering wheel. It was unusual for him to lose his cool.

"No one's going to die." Mark said calmly, looking at Grey sideways.

"What's this about?"

"Nothing." He grumbled, starting the truck.

"It's not NOTHING. What is it about?" he said more sternly.

"We've had worse odds than this." Mark reiterated.

Grey sighed. "Seraphine."

"What about her?"

"She had a vision, the day they left. She told me that one of us wouldn't make it back, and I know it's going to be me." He sighed, pulling over on the shoulder of the road.

"You have the babies and Megan. I have nothing, and no one." He looked at Mark and smiled.

"I just want to be back with Molly. So it HAS to be me."

"It can't be you." Mark said.

"I miss her every day. There is nothing for me here."

Mark sighed. They didn't need this shit right now.

He couldn't have Grey falling apart on him. Not now, when they were this close.

"I know you miss her. But this isn't your time. Or mine. I can feel it in my bones."

"You don't know that, if it comes down to it, it will be me. You have too much to lose."

"No one is fucking dying here." Mark said loudly.

"That's what YOU say."

"If you don't stop this shit I'm gonna kill you myself." Mark grumbled.

"Well whatever," Grey replied. "Let's rock and roll."

He drove towards the house.

"TOMMOROW NIGHT, IF SHE DOESN'T COME OUT, I'M GOING IN."

"We said two nights. We've waited this long. Don't ruin this. Give the girl a chance to see what she can do. She knows the house and the guards."

"Two days, that's all." Grey said flatly.

Mark starred out the window, as Grey drove. He couldn't believe that Grey had carried this with him all these weeks, and not said a damn thing to him.

He was ready to die for all of them, just like he always had, except this time he would purposely sacrifice himself to make sure Seraphine's vision worked in his favor.

Mark was pissed that she would even tell him something like this, knowing he would take it to heart. Knowing it could affect everything, including any judgement call he made. It was enough to make you wonder.

Raven was locked into her room once again, with Josephine. As she did every night, as soon as the door locked, she came and sat next to Raven and held her hand.

Raven picked her up and held her close. She had grown to love her.

"I met your Daddy today." Raven whispered to her. Josephine starred at her intently, understanding every word.

"I'm going to get us out of here. Tommorow night."

Raven watched the window in the door, when she was sure no one was watching she stuffed a few outfits into the back pack, and some of Josie's clothes and one of her Sippie cups.

She placed it under the bed, out of site.

Once she had rocked Josephine to sleep Raven put on the revealing top and bottom, she had purchased at the store earlier that day.

It was a white lace top that was very skimpy, and barely covered her breasts, and the bottom, a white lace g- string, Just as Anita had instructed her. It contrasted her tan body nicely.

She had formulated a plan. Raven knew the Greg had been watching her for weeks, every time she danced to pass the time.

She had led him on a little. Mainly out of boredom but hopefully it would prove to be effective now.

She kept telling herself all she had to do was to get outside to the backyard. Raven thought over her plan. The guard in front of her door had never left, when she had asked for the pizza.

She had seen the other guard, Mitch, as he had called him, hand the pizza off to Greg, when the door had been open. She thought that he was the one that got the pizza, the way he had complained.

Raven tapped on the window. Greg slid the door open.

"Yes?"

"Hi" she said.

"Hi," he replied suspiciously.

"You need something?"

"Some company…" she smiled.

"What do you mean?" Greg said nervously.

"Well I know that you have been watching me."

"Don't say that." he demanded.

"It's ok…" she whispered. "I won't tell. I like it."

Greg starred at her.

She backed away from the window so he could see her better.

She did look good, in that skimpy outfit. He HAD been watching her. His mouth fell open when he saw the new outfit.

Night after night, every time she danced, he had watched her bend over, it made him rock hard.

Greg had been thinking of going in while she slept, and just tearing that ass up.

"Can I get a pizza?" she asked.

"It's kinda late." He replied.

"Well how about tomorrow night then?" She smiled sweetly and leaned towards the opening.

"Why don't you open the door?"

"I'm not supposed to." He replied quietly, glancing up the steps nervously. They were all forbidden to even hold a conversation with her, but he had been fantasizing about her, and she did look good.

"Come on... your name's Greg right?"

As if she didn't already know. Raven heard them call each other on the walkie talkie's.

"Come in here and dance with me. It's so lonely here." She looked up at him with the most pitiful look she could muster.

"Just for a little while..... she begged. I haven't had any contact with anyone. My shoulders are hurting. I need them rubbed." Raven pouted now.

Greg glanced up the stairs, to make sure Mitch didn't see him. The upstairs door was closed. He unlocked the door and stepped inside, closing it behind him.

"Rub my shoulders for a minute..." Raven stated, turning her back towards him. He looked down at her g string and thanked his lucky stars.

Greg slowly rubbed her shoulders and her neck. She moved her head from side to side. "mmmm that feels so good."

He could feel himself getting excited.

"You have a beautiful body." Greg whispered, as Raven turned around to face him. She put her arms around his neck moving against his body. She could feel him pressing against her as he pulled her to him.

"I've been watching you too." She whispered in his ear.

She had him right where she wanted him.

"Greg, are you part of this organization?"

"Yes ma'am he said, born and raised." They swayed to the music.

"You must be very important, have you ever killed anyone?" she asked, rubbing his shoulders and arms.

"Just people who don't want to be true to the cause." He whispered in her ear.

"What about the girl, what's going to happen to her?"

"Some kind of sacrifice." He replied as he rubbed his hands down her lower back and buttocks.

"What kind of sacrifice?" Raven asked, kissing his neck.

"Why so many questions?" he asked abruptly pulling back.

"I'm fascinated by you, and I want to know what you do. You're so strong, and handsome." Her Hands rubbed his shoulders, and neck. She pulled him close again. "No one tells me anything."

"Ok..." he said, feeling flattered.

"They are going to sacrifice the little bitch, so the priestess can rise to power. It's an offering to the dark lord. It's what we do. Anita the Priestess, runs this church. In order for it to continue to get stronger, a sacrifice has to be made. Didn't you read your manual?"

"Yes, I did, but I can understand it better when you explain it." He beamed.

"Ok, so she needs the girl, to rise to power. It has to be someone related to her. She doesn't matter anyway. She is just a pain in the ass."

"Oh I see," she whispered in his ear, as her blood ran cold. She rubbed her hands over his manhood as he moaned. She had to be sure he was one of them, and not an innocent bystander. Now she knew. She had no more use for him tonight, and this was the fastest way to be rid of him.

Unzipping his pants, she took him in her hand and stroked up and down. Raven had all the information she needed.

He moaned and came quickly. He certainly wasn't expecting that.

"Damn girl, you didn't have to make me do that." He complained.

"I wanted to fuck you. She said we would be able to fuck you, me and Mitch."

"Who said that?" Raven asked.

"Anita. She said as soon as the kid dies. It was supposed to be Misha, but she had to go and die." He threw his hands up in annoyance.

He made her sick, but she retained the smile on her face.

"Is that so?"

"That's what the Priestess said."

"Well there's always tomorrow. We can send him for pizza, and then you can come in and we can have some fun." He smiled, his crooked rotten teeth exposed. It sounded like a great idea to him.

"Alright. I'll be here. Don't think you ain't gonna give me that sweet pussy tomorrow."

"Then you better get me that pizza." She smiled sweetly.

He pinched her nipple hard, and turned around and walked out, slamming the door behind himself. She rubbed the back of her hand over her lips, trying to rub his saliva off of her.

Raven felt disgusting.

She eased herself down on the rocking chair, looking at Josephine's sleeping form. She felt dirty. She starred at the floor. There was no other choice. She told herself.

Raven was doing it to save Josie, and that was all that mattered. It gave her little comfort on this night, as she hugged her knees to her chest.

There had been no man in her life, since she had been date raped in the motel the night she had almost ended her life. The life before Raven. Annie had died then, and Raven had saved her.

Now it was up to Raven to save Josephine, no matter what the cost.

She slipped into her sweat pants, a t- shirt and turned off the light. Raven curled up on the small bed and covered herself, up to her chin with the quilt.

She was shivering. Tomorrow would be the day. She would have to be brave. She didn't know why she had been picked. She was certainly not brave, yet she would do what needed to be done.

She thought of the man in the store. Mark. Raven prayed he would really be there when she came out. She had no further plan than the back yard. He had to be there, that was all there was to it.

Raven thought back to the dream of the field. She had been chosen for this. Somehow this realization made her feel braver.

Knowing that they would sacrifice Josephine, an innocent child, and then kill her too. She knew what she had to do.

Mark and Grey waited anxiously all night. There had been nothing, no movement, no sign from Raven. After sunrise they each took turns sleeping a few hours. Grey woke Mark at sunset.

"The crazy dude left." He said, referring to George, who had stormed out of the house in an uproar.

"He was screaming at Anita about searching for a girl, and about Lupe slipping through his fingers again. He was pissed." Grey laughed.

"One down."

As he did every night after eight, Mark sat on the inside of the wall and waited, only this night Grey sat next to him. This was the night they had been waiting for.

She was either coming out, or they were going in. One way or another, this part of the journey would end tonight.

"You're like a brother to me." Grey said to him.

"Shut up, you're not dying here." Mark whispered.

Grey shook his head and smiled. He loved that asshole. In a way he was glad that it would be over soon, and he was grateful for good friends, and for most of the like he had led.

A few moments later the door opened and Anita stormed out the door, talking loudly on her cell phone.

"I don't know where he went. I have a meeting in two hours. I have just enough time to get there. I need your support."

She paced now.

"Yes," she said to the voice on the other end. "I'm meeting up with the men from Texas tonight, to confirm the ritual."

Mitch brought the car around.

"You stay here." She commanded. "I'm going alone."

"Two down." Grey said with a smile. This was a bonus.

The moon had come out and was full tonight, so they had to retreat further into the shadows. It was after ten, when they saw one of the guards come into the kitchen get a drink and leave again. There was also the guard out front, so they knew there had to be one more.

Then there was the Albino, who was unaccounted for. Grey didn't want to leave here without killing Anita, but they had to get the baby out. They had made a pact to wait till midnight. If she didn't come out by then, they were going in.

He hoped by some miracle she could get out, so there would be no shooting.

Inside the basement Raven tapped on the window. It slid open almost immediately.

"Hey" Greg said. He had been thinking of her all day.

He couldn't wait to get inside her. He knew her type, the teasing bitch kind. He had, had a few like her. He had shown all of them who the man was, just like he would show her.

"Are we getting that pizza?" She asked.

"Absolutely," he said. He didn't even shut the window, but yelled up the steps.

"MITCH" The door flew open.

"What man?"

The lady wants a pizza."

"Fuck dude, it's late." Mitch complained.

"Pizza place stays open till 11."

"I'm not going out this late to get a fucking pizza." Mitch complained.

"I'll buy you a pack of smokes. How 'bout that?" Greg bribed.

Mitch came down the stairs.

"Why? What are you up to?"

"I'm going to fuck her." He whispered proudly.

"No way." Mitch replied.

"Yeah." He puffed out his chest. She said so.

"Do you think I could get a turn?" Mitch asked.

"When you get back. I'm getting her first though."

"What about the kid?" Mitch asked.

"What do you mean?" Greg asked. His face wrinkled. He had heard rumors of his charges.

"You think I could have a turn at her too?" he smiled slyly.

"Man, the kid?" Greg laughed. "You are a sick fuck, but whatever, I don't give a shit."

"I'll be back in 30," he yelled as he took the steps, two at a time, slamming the cellar door.

He walked out the front door, and told Carl he was going for pizza.

They knew no one was supposed to leave the house, if Anita and George were both gone. "Go man hurry up before she comes back, and bring me back a couple burgers."

"Damn I wasn't planning on running all over town." He bitched as he pulled out of the driveway, unaware that Grey watched him from the top off the wall. He moved his way around to the back yard, and told Mark.

Something was about to happen, Grey could feel it in his bones.

Raven had spent the day fashioning a glass shard that she had broken off of the tray in the small fridge.

Greg entered the room. He walked over, and grabbed Raven by the back of her hair, pulling her head back. He bit her neck and ran his yellow stained tongue over her cheek. He kissed her hard and unzipped his pants.

Greg looked over at the sleeping child in the bed, and rubbed himself. Raven felt the bile rising in her throat. She had overheard the entire conversation with Mitch.

"Hey slow down…" She whispered.

She pulled him over to the bed, and pushed him down, diverting his attention away from the sleeping child, by rubbing against him. His hips began to gyrate against hers.

He pulled out a condom.

"Put this on me." Raven fumbled around with it, until he became impatient and put it on himself.

He grabbed her breasts and squeezed them hard. Greg reached between her legs and ripped her panties in half.

Ravens heart pounded so hard she was afraid he would hear. Greg flipped her over, pulled her down on him, and started to plunge into her. Raven suppressed the urge to vomit.

She looked over at Josephine, who was sleeping soundly, as a tear ran down her face. She reached behind her and grabbed the shard.

Raven remembered Greg's face, when he had talked about killing Josephine, calling her a little bitch, and promising Mitch he could have her, when he returned. He squeezed her breasts harder, as Raven winced with pain.

He pulled her face to his.

"When this is over I'm gonna fuck you again, and so is Mitch. You little whore. We might even let the Albino fuck you."

He laughed, and grabbed her hips and pushed her up and down faster, moaning loudly. He was a muscular man and she hoped she had what it took to incapacitate him.

Raven was starting to panic, she told herself that all she had to do was get out of the house, and they would be there to help her. She prayed they would really be there. She couldn't lose her nerve now.

Raven leaned over and started to grind her hips harder. As soon as Greg closed his eyes, she plunged the shard into the side of his neck, over and over. The blood splattered on her face and chest.

He blinked several times, and tried to hold his hand over the spurting hole.

Raven was up and pulled her pants on. She wiped the blood with his shirt and threw it on him in disgust. She yanked on her shirt, and grabbed the backpack out from under the bed. She watched the color drain out of Greg's face. Raven reached down and grabbed the Shard, shoving the bloody thing in her pocket.

He was trying to sit up, gurgling. She grabbed Josephine, and ran for the door. It opened easily. The key was still in the lock. Her heart pounded loudly.

She could still hear him making strange noises. He was probably getting up right now and coming after her, she thought. Raven slammed the basement door, and locked It.

Josephine starred at her wide eyed not making a sound, as if she knew. Hoisting her up further, as the child clutched onto her neck, hiding her face.

Raven ran up the step, two at a time. At the top she took a deep breath and slowly opened the door.

There was no one. Her heart pounded. Suddenly, she was having some kind of flash back.

A memory from the night in the hotel. She was close to hyperventilating. Josephine's soft hand, on her cheek snapped her out of it. Their eyes met, and she knew she had to keep going.

Suddenly she thought she heard footsteps, and ran for the back door. Mark spotted her as soon as she turned the corner of the hallway. He was on his feet running towards her, his weapon drawn.

Grey close behind, packing an arsenal.

She tried to unlock the door, her hands slippery, and still covered in blood. Finally, Mark ripped the door open and pulled her out.

Tears ran down her face, as Mark pulled her to the wall. Sobbing she handed Josephine to Mark. Grey grabbed Raven by her waist and hoisted her over.

Grey went up next. Mark handed him the baby, and watched them disappear over the wall.

Grey started the truck, just as the security lights in the compound came on. He watched Mark's large form come over the wall. He jumped into the truck, just as it was backing up.

Once on the road, Grey floored the truck, but slowed down when he saw headlights coming toward them. They recognized Mitch coming back with pizza. Once he was out of site, he floored it again. "You have to pull over." Mark said.

Grey pulled over onto the shoulder, wondering what was going on.

Mark jumped out and yanked open the door. He pulled Josephine into his arms and hugged her to him. Her arms went around his neck. Tears flowed freely down his face.

"My baby girl….your alive." He tried not to squeeze her too hard. Grey lowered his gaze. He smiled. A large lump had formed in his throat. He fought back his own tears. She looked so much like Sam. He thanked God in a silent prayer. They hadn't had words in a long time.

He got back onto the highway. Mark had Josephine in his arms, and had managed to pull the seatbelt around them both.

Grey watched Raven in the mirror. She had no color in her face. Once he was sure no one followed he pulled over, and opened the back door. She cringed, pulling away as he leaned in.

"Are you alright?" Grey asked. "Is that your blood?"

She didn't answer. Grey pulled her shirt up to check for bleeding, as she started swinging at him. He held her arms over her head with one Massive hand, and once he was satisfied that she wasn't physically injured, he climbed in beside her.

He exchanged glances with Mark, who strapped Josephine back in alone. He got into the driver's side. They had to keep moving.

"It's not her blood. She's in shock though." Grey said.

Raven was shaking, her lips quivering.

Grey retrieved a blanket and covered her, pulling it up to her neck.

"It's ok, you're safe now." His deep voice resonated. She was breathing harder, and making small sobbing noises. She started to hyperventilate, tears streaming down her face.

He pulled her to him, and wrapped his arms around her, holding her tightly. She fought him for a few moments, but exhaustion finally took over, and she went limp. "Jesus," Mark said. "Is she breathing?"

"Yeah, she just wore herself out."

They drove for hours. Mark watching the road, and Josephine, who had finally fallen asleep. Towards daylight they pulled into a Walmart.

Grey waited in the Jeep, while Mark went inside and purchased supplies for Josie and clean clothes for Raven, and a few groceries.

He entered the vehicle, started the engine, and headed to a motel, on the outskirts of town. Grey carried Raven inside, and sat her down on the bed. She was still shaking.

He pulled her toward the bathroom, and she started to fight him again. He grabbed her shoulders.

"It's ok your safe." Raven continued to slap at him, he finally pulled her into his massive arms again, and restrained her. She was small compared to him, as were most people.

She stopped fighting, and started to sob. Grey pulled her tighter, and patted her back. "It's ok", he whispered again. "You're going to be ok."

Mark watched him from across the room. Wondering what this would bring. He thought of Seraphine and what she had said.

"The Raven is dark but light."

Grey loosened his arms around Raven, and led her into the bathroom. He towered over her, but she didn't seem to notice anymore. When he pulled her bloody shirt off of her, she sat like a stone.

His large arms lifted her into the bath tub, so he could shower the blood off of her. She still wore her bra. He removed it from behind and covered her with the small hand towel. As he worked he moved the towel to hide the areas, on her that were private.

He shampooed the blood out of her hair. He noticed the small birthmark on the back of her neck right by her hairline. It resembled a three point star. Grey washed her face, and arms. The blood had dried and he had to scrub it away, trying his best to avert his eyes, and to be a gentleman.

Once finished, he dried her off, and pulled one of his clean white T shirts over her head.

He sat her down on the toilet and pulled the sweat pants that Mark had purchased over her feet. He helped her stand and pulled them up, careful not to touch her skin. Grey led her to the bed and tucked the blanket around her.

He sighed, and watched her for a few moments, till she fell asleep.

Grey walked over to Mark, and Josephine's sleeping form on his lap. He sat down across from him. He looked at the sleeping child.

"She's beautiful." He whispered.

As soon as the words left his lips, she sat up, and opened her eyes, looking directly into his.

He felt a warmth pass through him, that brought tears to his eyes.

Grey felt a peace, and joy that he had never felt before. Mark watched the interaction, and somehow he knew that something was at work, something bigger that all of them.

They made their pallets, for the night. Mark and Josephine, by the bathroom side, and Grey on the floor, between the bed and the door.

Raven was still asleep.

"Are you good?" Grey asked.

"Yes. I'm good." He replied, as he turned off the lamp.

Grey woke during the night, when he heard Raven cry out. He reached up, and switched on the small lamp by the bed.

Raven starred at him.

"Easy." He said, holding his hand out in front of him, in case she started slapping him again. She had whacked him a few good ones.

"I'm Grey, and you know Mark."

"Where are my clothes?" she asked quietly, pulling the blanket around herself.

"They are soaking. There was a lot of blood. You have clothes on." He told her.

She looked down at herself, and realized she was clothed. Raven lay back against the pillow and pulled the blanket up again.

"You were covered in blood. I had to make sure it wasn't yours." He said softly.

She rolled onto her side to face him.

"Where are we?"

"I'm not sure. We have been driving for hours. I think we are near Canjilon."

"Is Josephine ok?"

"Yes, you saved her." Grey said quietly, nodding towards the floor, where she slept in her father's arms.

Raven glanced at the other side of the floor.

She nodded her head. Tears began to flow again. This was a good thing.

"I did terrible things." She sobbed.

"No," he said. "You did what you had to do to get out."

"They were going to kill us both." She cried.

"And worse than that..."

Her eyes met his. He finally got a good look at her. She was so small, and beautiful.

"You're safe now."

He reached over and took her hand in his. It seemed to swallow it up.

"You should probably get some sleep." Grey said.

"I'm scared. Are you sure they don't know where we are?"

"Yes I'm sure." He really wasn't sure of anything, but he knew no harm would come to her. He would make sure of that. Grey knew they hadn't been followed. There was time to rest.

"Can I turn off the light?" he asked.

"yes." she replied.

He flipped off the lamp, and got back onto his pallet, on the floor beside the bed.

"Thank you for helping me." Raven whispered.

"Your welcome." The deep voice whispered in the dark

"Grey?"

"Yes?"

"Can I please lay with you? I'm so scared."

His eyes were wide in the dark. He was no saint by any means, but he hadn't had any contact with a female, in a long time. Grey starred into the dark.

He was scared now.

Grey exhaled slowly, trying to slow his heart rate down, while Raven waited for his response.

It was ridiculous, he thought. She was so small, in comparison to him, and he was afraid to lay with her.

"Grey?" she whispered.

"Ok." The words left his mouth, before he knew it.

He felt her put her pillow on the floor beside his. She lay down next to him, and pulled the blanket up around herself.

"The floor is hard, did you want me to come up there with you?" he asked.

"No I feel safer down here."

He smiled to himself. So did he.

When her breathing changed he knew she was asleep, but for him sleep didn't come. He tried to picture Molly's face, but he couldn't picture it.

He got up and went to the bathroom. When he was done he pulled up Ravens bloody clothes, and tossed them in the wastebasket. The stains would never come out. It would be better if she didn't see them. The shard fell onto the floor at his feet. He bent down to pick it up.

"What the fuck." He mumbled to himself.

He tucked it into his bag, and returned to the pallet on the floor. He stretched out and was grateful to not be scrunched up in a vehicle.

He folded his arms under his head, just before Raven rolled over and nuzzled herself into his side.

His heart pounded. He tried to calm himself by thinking of other things. It was not a sexual thing. He wasn't sure what he was feeling. Since Josephine had looked into his eyes his feelings had gone crazy.

He didn't know what was going on. Grey lay in the dark and listened to Raven's soft breathing. For the first time in years, everything was right in his life. Finally in the early morning hours he fell asleep.

George was the first to return to the house. He knew there was a problem when he pulled down the gravel drive and saw the flood lights on.

He eased the car, onto the side, and walked cautiously up to the house.

Carl stood just inside the front door.

"What happened here?" he asked.

Carl swallowed hard.

Greg is dead.

"What the fuck do you mean he's dead? What happened?"

"Mitch went to get pizza and something happened in the basement."

George was already heading into the house and down the basement steps.

He smelled the blood before he got to the bottom.

It was a gruesome scene.

Ravens entire bed was covered with blood. Greg's lifeless body was grotesquely hanging off the side, obviously bled out. George looked him over.

He had several large puncture marks on the side of his neck, not to mention his pants were down.

"What the fuck." George said, pulling back the covers of the toddler bed. Empty. Anita was going to have a stroke. Raven was gone, and so was the kid.

George headed back up the steps, to find Carl.

Carl was still sitting in the same place.

"Where is Mitch?"

"He hauled ass. He said he was leaving before you, and the priestess got back."

"What happened here?"

"Apparently Greg decided to make a go at Raven. He said Greg was gonna do her first, and then Mitch, and the kid too.

"Looks like she didn't want to." George stated.

"Where's Francis?"

"Still locked in the cage."

"Did you call her?"

"HELL NO." Carl replied, as he held his weapon close. He knew George was a loose cannon.

George walked to his room, scratching his head. She was going to flip out. He stood for a moment, deciding his next course of action.

He packed a small bag, and headed for his car.

He thought about letting Francis loose before he left, just to make things even more interesting, but then decided against it, mainly because he just didn't feel like dealing with the retarded fucker.

George got into his car, and called Anita, explaining the situation. There was silence on the other end.

"Did Mitch take the baby?" she asked quietly.

"Why the hell would he do that?" George asked.

"He had some previous things...., involving children."

"Things?" George inquired.

"Charges. He's a pervert."

"Now that is just fucking sick." George announced.

"You have to find him, and get the baby back."

"How do you know Raven didn't take her?"

"I don't." she hissed.

"Go and find out. I'm in Texas. I'll be heading back tonight."

He was surprised that she didn't sound more upset.

Something was definitely up.

What he didn't know was that the elders had voted, and decided that Megan was the only true descendant of Anita. Without her there would be no ascension.

The baby would no longer be needed, unless they required leverage to get Megan to do what they needed. Anita was sure that Megan would gladly trade her own life, for Josephine's.

Once she explained it to George, he headed off in the direction Mitch had taken. He knew the car. The rest would be easy.

If he had done anything sexual to the little girl he would make him suffer more than usual. He was a killer but he had his standards.

Carl was glad to see him drive away, thankful that he hadn't killed him.

Mark woke up first. He was surprised to see Grey and Raven on the floor. His arms around her, as they both slept.

He wished that he had some way to contact Megan. To let her know their daughter was alive. In the meantime they had to keep moving.

Grey woke up next. He felt her before he opened his eyes. For a moment he didn't know what to do. He lay there trying to orient himself to the moment.

Then it all came back to him as he awoke fully. He didn't know exactly when he had pulled her into his arms, he remembered her crying in her sleep, and he guessed it was then. She looked small in comparison to him, as she held on to his massive arm with both her hands.

He started to doze off again, when he felt her stirring. He opened his eyes, and they met hers. The gaze held for a moment, as the warm feeling came over him again. Grey felt like he knew her, not just now, but somehow before this moment. It was a strange feeling. He had never felt it before.

She must have felt it too, because she broke the gaze and jumped up, wrapped in her blanket.

"Good morning." He whispered.

"Morning." She grumbled.

It was awkward at best.

Josephine slept, on the other pallet.

Mark sat at the table studying a map.

"Good morning." He said as she walked by.

"Morning."

She headed into to the bathroom, with her bag.

Raven showered and scrubbed herself vigorously, trying to put the incident of the previous night out of her mind.

She had taken a life to save a life.

Raven dressed, and pulled her hair up into a bun. Looking at herself in the mirror, as she wondered what the future would bring.

She still felt afraid. In the short time she had spent with Anita she had come to realize that her grasp was long. No one was safe. Then there was George, who had asked her to come back, in return for Josephine's life.

She had orchestrated her own plan, and had managed to get out without his help.

Raven was scared out of her mind. They would be coming for her. She returned to the room. Grey had made the bed and cleaned up the pallet. He was fully dressed.

"I'm starving to death. Is there any food?" Raven said.

Mark and Grey starred at each other, and both stifled laughter.

They went to a small diner for breakfast. Raven ordered scrambled eggs with cheese for Josie. It was her favorite. She sat with Raven and held on to her arm.

"I didn't thank you properly." Mark said.

"You saved my daughter. I can never repay you for that, but I thank you from the bottom of my heart."

Raven smiled, a brief smile, and nodded.

"Your welcome."

She wondered if she had fulfilled her purpose here on earth, now that Josephine was safe.

"I don't really know her," Mark said. He explained how she had been taken at birth. My wife hasn't even seen her since then. She is a twin. She has a brother named Sam."

"Do they look alike?" Raven asked.

"Yes Grey answered, very much alike. He's a little hippie. Blond hair, blue eyes, just like her.

"Why isn't she talking?" Mark asked.

"She doesn't talk." Raven replied.

"When I got there they said she had never talked, but I think she understands everything. She is very smart."

Josephine nudged Ravens arm.

"She has to go to the bathroom."

Grey followed them, and waited outside the door. They returned to the table together.

They made small talk, until Grey asked her about her family.

"Do you want us to take you to your family?" He had asked.

"There is no one." She replied.

"What about your parents?"

"They are dead. I have nowhere to go. Anita and George will find me, and they will kill me."

She said matter of factly. Convinced that she had done what she was sent to do.

"No." Grey said. "That is not going to happen. I'm not going to let it."

"You can't stop it. If she doesn't kill me, George will. He hates me because I stopped him from killing Lupe."

"We aren't going to let that happen." Mark said.

Raven wasn't convinced. They finished breakfast and got back on the road.

Megan awoke suddenly. As Seraphine shook her

"We have to go."

"Why? What's wrong?" She was already scrambling around trying to pack up her few belongings.

Seraphine was pale. Her worst fears had come true. Until now she hadn't understood her vision.

"I can't tell you now, but please we have to go. You must trust me."

Megan picked Sam up off his bed, and wrapped him in his blanket.

Sleeve was not there when she came out. It was still dark out, as they made their way to the back of the camp.

She followed Seraphine, while clutching the child to her chest.

"What about Red bird? Does he know what's happening?"

Seraphine shushed her.

"Not now girl, we must go."

Lupe waited with three horses.

No one spoke, as they moved on, through the dark night, further into the desert.

The night was cold and somewhere in the distance a wolf pack howled.

Megan was scared, but they rode on through the night. The wind had picked up, and it started to snow.

Megan wrapped Sam up tighter in his blankets. She pulled her jacket closer around herself.

As the daylight crept over the horizon, the mountain range came into view.

Seraphine led her horse through a small clearing, into a pass. The others followed.

A few moments later, a large cave opened up. They unmounted and led the horses inside, out of the cold.

Seraphine made a small fire, and they warmed their hands. Megan watched her, waiting for her to speak.

"Seraphine," what is happening? Please you have to tell me."

Seraphine sat down beside her, and picked up her hand. She clung tightly to it.

Shaking her head. "I have had a vision. The clearest one I have ever had. The dark is coming. I have seen it's face." She cried openly now.

"What is it?" Megan asked. "Who is he?"

"It isn't a man at all, but some kind of Demon. It once was a woman, but now it has taken on another form.

Megan intinctively knew it was Anita.

"How did she find us." Megan asked.

Seraphine shook her head.

"There is one who has turned against you, against all of us."

Mark drove most of the day. One small town after another passed them by.

"What's the plan?" Grey finally asked.

"I have to go and find Megan, and Sam."

"You mean, WE."

"No I mean Me. I am not risking Josephine's life or Ravens. I have to go in alone."

"YOU'RE NOT GOING IN THERE ALONE." Grey stated.

"Yes, I am, and I need to ask a favor of you. I know you're not going to like it, but I am trusting you, to watch over my daughter until I come back for her.

Grey sighed. He didn't like it. But he knew it made sense. He knew the desert was no place for a child. It was also the biggest honor he could ever have. To be entrusted with Josephine.

Either way he didn't feel good about it, but reluctantly agreed. Mark rented a room for two weeks. It was small and shabby but clean, and off the beaten path.

There was no way anyone would come looking for them here, and it was in walking distance to a small grocery. There would be no car, so no one would even suspect them.

Mark left Grey a bundle of cash. He was still running on the bag of money that Megan had originally gotten out of the bank in Florida. There was enough to live on for quite a while and enough to buy a car if he didn't come back.

They both knew the risks. If Mark didn't return in two weeks they were to buy a car and head to the fortress. Grey's fortress.

Mark kissed Josephine goodbye, with tears in his eyes. He had only just found her, and was leaving her again.

"I have to find your momma." He whispered. She smiled at him as if she understood.

Her small hand reaching up to touch his face. As she connected with him he felt a powerful surge run through his body. The desert trail came into view, and several landmarks, like a memory.

 He saw a mountain and a cave and Seraphine. A figure in red appeared. He was unable to see his face. Megan was screaming.

Suddenly the vision was gone. He was standing in the shabby room with Grey and Raven. She had taken her hand away from his face.

"What the hell was that?" Grey asked.

"I don't know…as soon as she touched me I felt this wave of energy, and then I saw Serapine and Megan, there was a man but I couldn't make it out. I have to go, NOW." Somehow he knew that the images he had seen had not happened yet. He knew where to go. She had shown him the way.

He knew time was of the essence. He starred at Josephine who starred back at him and nodded. There was something about her. Whatever was evil was out there, she was the good. He didn't have time to sort it all out now, but he knew.

They said their goodbyes, and Mark drove away.

Raven and Grey finished chips and sandwiches, left over from lunch. Josephine ate a bowl of mac and cheese. She fell asleep shortly after dinner.

Raven lay her in the playpen Mark had bought the previous day. It was a better bed than the floor.

She sat next to Grey on the small couch. After several attempts he threw the remote on the table.

"There are no stations."

Raven nodded.

"I killed a man." She blurted out, as tears sprang from her eyes.

"I figured as much." Grey replied.

"You figured as much?" she said angrily.

"Yes. There was a lot of blood and it wasn't yours."

"Brilliant deduction." She hissed.

Grey sighed. He didn't really know what else to do.

"Well?" she said.

"Well what?"

"Is that all you have to say about it?"

"I don't know what you want me to say." He replied quietly.

She wiped the tears that just kept coming.

"What happened in there?"

Through her sobs Raven told him of the Guards and the things they had said, about Josephine and their sick plans. She described the weapon she had forged, and told how she used it, to get out.

"I'm sorry you had to go through it, and that you had to do such a thing, but you saved Josephine and yourself, and that's what's really important here."

She blurted out the night she had been raped and left in the hotel, and how she had driven Granny's car over the embankment trying to end it all.

He sat and listened intently, as she spoke of the dream, and the strange vision she had had after, in the room.

Grey shook his head, as if he understood.

"Everything that happened sounds like it led you here in this direction. Maybe you were meant to save Josephine."

"YES, I was."

"It's a good thing that you did. The cult is just evil. They would have sacrificed her to keep the bloodline going. It's like a fight of good against evil. Anita destroys every family she touches in one way or another."

"I'm tired." Raven announced. She felt as if every ounce of energy had been drained out of her, now that she had confessed everything.

"Where are we going to sleep?"

"This couch pulls out into a bed." Grey stated.

"OK, well I'm not a prostitute."

"What?" He was appalled.

"You heard me."

He starred at her in disbelief.

"I did, but I don't understand why you would say that. No one thinks that."

He didn't understand why she was so defensive.

"Just so we are clear."

"It made her feel uncomfortable to be in the same room with him. She had no real experience with men, only the bad.

His size frightened her too. He was a giant compared to her. She knew she would never be able to fight him off.

He swallowed hard, and walked over to the small sink for a drink of water.

"I'll sleep over on the floor, and you take the bed." He said cautiously.

"That's fine with me." She slammed the cushion onto the floor and pulled the bed out. She threw herself on it, and rolled over, facing the wall.

"Did you want a blanket?" Grey asked, pulling two blankets from the closet.

The room had gotten colder since the sun had set. The heat didn't seem to work.

He threw the blanket lightly on the bed. Raven snatched it, and rolled back over.

"What's your problem?" Grey finally asked, annoyed with her actions.

"I don't have a problem, except that I have to be in the same room with you."

She replied sarcastically.

"I'm sorry. Unfortunately there is nowhere else for me to go. I would go sleep in the car, but there isn't one." He replied lightly.

"Great, what a comedian. Your wife must be so proud."

Grey starred at her. He could feel his pulse beating in his neck. He tried to control the anger that was rising in him, Telling himself that she didn't know, and it was merely a poor choice of words. He squeezed the blanket in is hands as hard as he could.

Raven starred at him.

"What?" she asked cautiously. The look on his face was not pleasant. She knew she had gone too far.

"My wife is dead. My daughter is dead. They bleed to death in the snow. So your little spoiled ass isn't the only one who lost something."

He spoke quietly, almost a whisper, to keep from losing his self- control, but she heard every word.

Raven starred at him.

"I'm sorry. I didn't know." She sat up on the end of the bed starring at him.

He starred back at her, feeling stupid for even disclosing it. He didn't owe anyone an explanation, and he certainly wasn't looking for pity. Not from her.

"Grey,.....please, I am truly sorry. I shouldn't have acted like that. I was scared to be alone in the room with you. I don't..... have very good experiences with men."

She attempted a small smile.

Grey shook his head. "Ok. I get it."

He was still angry.

Laying down on his pallet, he had made on the floor, he asked her to turn off the light.

Raven switched off the small lamp on the night stand.

They lay in the dark, each lost in their own thoughts.

"I would never hurt you." Grey said.

"I'm not that kind of guy."

"I know." Raven replied. "I am truly sorry. Please forgive me."

"I know I'm kind of a big guy, and I look intimidating, but I have never hurt a woman in my life."

He was offended that she would even think such a thing.

Raven smiled in the dark, thinking of his words. "Kind of a big guy."

"I didn't mean to accuse you." She said.

He started to doze off a few minutes later.

"Grey." He flinched awake.

"What?"

"Can you come lay with me? I'm scared."

He starred into the dark. His heart pounding. He really didn't want to. He was still pissed off.

He sighed, and stood up.

"OK." He grabbed his pillow and moved into the bed beside her.

Twenty minutes later, when he was almost asleep, he felt her small hand slip into his.

In her playpen, Josephine smiled.

The men from Texas, and the elders of the cult began to arrive just after sunset.

Anita hadn't come back yet, and George was surprised. He let the guests in and showed them to the large sitting room.

She arrived a few moments later. George met her outside and told her that he had found Mitch and that he didn't have the child, and had not had a chance to touch her, now he never would.

"Raven must have taken her." He deducted.

Anita simply smiled at him. "We don't need her after all. The men are coming. They will be here soon. Carl, get this damn mess cleaned up. Block off the basement, so my people don't see what a mess you all have made, while I was gone." She paced picking up small items and moving them around.

"It's ridiculous." She stated and gave him the hand, like he had disturbed her garden party. He saw that mad glimmer in her eyes. She really was crazy, hell she may have had some sort of breakdown. He had never seen her like this before. "What are you talking about?" George asked trying not to raise his voice. Although her security was gone, the rest of the crazies were coming. It was a week early.

"I am having a ceremony tonight, George." He hated when she enunciated his name.

"It is very important. You of all people should know this." Her voice was shrill.

"Yes, I know, priestess." He said bowing to her, getting back into her good graces quickly. Although she had no security left, except Carl, he knew the men that were coming. He wanted no part of them. He would deal with her later, one on one.

"I will prepare the house." George stated.

Anita rushed down the hall to her room. She bathed, and perfumed herself, exhilarating at the thought of the ritual. After, she slipped on her ceremonial robe, and placed the pendant around her neck.

While she prepared the guest arrived and were ushered into the great hall. There had been many ceremonies, they were usually the same. George saw some new faces. New recruits he imagined.

An hour later, when she entered, everyone stood. It was a large room and easily accommodated the twenty two people. The two elders pushed the large table aside, and once the carpet was rolled up a giant pentagram came to life on the wooden floor.

It was carved meticulously, on the original floor. It had been there for many years. The chanting began just as George stepped into the back of the crowd.

He waited in the shadows of the room, deliberately hanging back. He was what he was, but he wanted no part of this devil mumbo jumbo. It gave him the creeps. He was a killer, but this made him uneasy. He had seen some things in this house. He was afraid that one day Anita would unleash something worse than all of them put together.

The Elders took turns speaking in a strange tongue, as they unfolded a table in the middle of the room. The man from Texas, also now in a robe walked up to Anita and pulled her robe over her head. He had been bathed and pampered by the elders.

As he helped her onto the table, the group began to chant, he stroked her body, and chanted along.

George watched in amusement. What a bunch of bullshit, he thought to himself.

Another man walked into the room, in a long red robe, with a hood. George didn't recognize him. He looked around the room.

Everyone else was accounted for. George counted the robed figures. There had been twenty two.

He always counted them. He liked to know who he was dealing with, and how many. Now there were twenty three. Watching as the man from Texas dropped his robe, George scowled. This was going to be another sick one.

The man continued to stroke Anita's body, over her breasts and between her legs. She writhed with pleasure as he rubbed harder entering his entire fist in her, and moving it in, and out quickly, in unison with the chanting.

After a few moments he pulled her to the edge of the table and entered her, his large cock thrusting into her. She ran her hands over her breasts, as one of the cloaked men poured what appeared to be blood, over her chest, and neck.

The Texan continued to thrust his hips. Suddenly the man in the red cloak moved behind him, and began to fondle his buttocks and his thighs. The man moaned as the cloaked figure entered him from behind, and all three thrust in unison.

George was watching intensely. This wasn't part of the ritual. It was always the same. Something bad was about to happen. He could feel it. Anita never deviated from the strict instructions of the rituals.

The Texan threw his head back, and just as the cloaked man came inside of him, George saw the flash of a blade, as he ran it across the man's exposed throat. Blood spurted on Anita, as the gurgling man started to fall forward.

The chanting became louder and louder. The red figure pushed the Texan aside, his limp corpse falling to the floor. He rubbed the blood all over Anita's bare body, as she continued to moan. She looked up at the hooded figure, and the smile left her face. She tried to sit up, but the cloaked man pushed her back down and entered her. He was large, much larger than the Albino.

She squirmed trying to get away. Several of the elders approached the altar, as more hooded men appeared, and formed a sort of circle around the two. The shadowy figures dropped their hoods, and the elders backed away.

 George starred at their faces, they were not really faces at all, but disfigured dark shadows, almost translucent. They were not of this world.

George ran for the basement, as he heard Anita's screams. He had seen enough, and had no desire to see who or what was under the red cloak.

George took the steps two at a time. He knew no one had seen him.

The screams were unimaginable now.

He opened the basement door, and grabbed the key off of the wall. Francis sat in the cage. He had been forgotten.

Greg usually fed him, and he hadn't shown up in several days. The water had run out, the day before. Sitting in his own excrement he waited, rocking his body back and forth.

He smelled the foul stench as soon as he stuck his head in.

"Jesus" he whispered. There was no time.

He couldn't stand the creepy bastard, but if he had any chance of getting out of the house alive he needed him.

George unlocked the door, and it creaked as he ripped it open.

"Francis," He said as he grabbed both his shoulders to get his attention.

"I need you to get up. We have to go. It's an emergency. We have to help the priestess."

The Albino stood.

"Help the priestess?" He repeated in his encumbered voice.

"Yes." Let's go. There are bad people in the house." For a split second as they headed up the steps he felt a pang of guilt, for what he was about to do. He needed a diversion, and Francis was all he had.

At the top of the steps the screams continued, but they had changed in some way. Francis moved when he heard the screams. Now they had changed.

They sounded almost like a low growl. Francis moved unusually fast as he entered the room. George watched as he dove through the circle of Archfiends.

He had no fear, because he didn't understand what they were. His feeble mind had no knowledge of such things.

Bodies were strewn about everywhere.

The elders, all dead. Body parts strewn about, and the stench of blood permeated the room. George, who had planned to run, was frozen in place watching the red cloak fall to the ground, empty.

At the same time, Anita sat up, and threw her legs over the side of the table. The Albino stood next to her, and smiled.

"George," He called, as the morphed eyes, of what was once Anita snapped in his direction.

He came running over, as if to help. The fiend starred at him for a moment. He picked up a robe and placed it over her shoulders, to cover her.

A low gnarl escaped her lips. George's heart beat in his throat. He knew there was no point in running. He helped her off the table. The things legs wobbled. Francis followed behind.

"George, where are we going."

"Quiet, Francis. Let me think."

George held an arm, as it headed for the door. Its spindly legs inching along as if it was just learning how to walk.

"Priestess, we need to put on some clothes." He said softly, trying not to antagonize the thing.

The neck creaked to the side, as it looked at him. The foul breath made his stomach turn, as he pulled a sun dress over its head.

The demonic voice that came out, was not Anita's, but a much deeper tone, and not of this world.

"I am Abbadon. You will serve me."

Mark drove to the edge of the desert, where his gut told him where they went in. Once the car was parked he hoisted the backpack on, and walked into the desert.

He walked for several miles. It was so dark he couldn't see two feet in front of his face. Although he had the compass, he decided it was futile, and sat down, covering himself with his blanket.

He slept on and off for a few hours, hearing the occasional wolf or coyote, howling in the distance. He woke up suddenly, and saw that the sun was rising. Mark stood and shook off his blanket. He ate a small handful of nuts and jerky, and downed a bottle of water.

He checked the compass and headed west. Redbird had told him only this that they would be heading west and that when it was all over he could find them there. Josephine had shown him the rest.

Three days later the oasis came into view. The sun beginning to set again.

Mark sweated profusely all day, and now that the temperature had dropped to 50 degrees, he was shivering in his wet clothes. For a moment he wasn't sure if it was really there, at all.

Before he could even reach the perimeter, the braves encircled him.

He told them who he was, as they led him inside, as the small tropical paradise unfolded in front of him. There was a pool of water with tropical plants all around, and a good sized garden to the left.

Mark anxiously waited, as the braves entered a tipi in the middle of the small makeshift village, they had fashioned inside the Oasis.

They returned, and waited as Kona stepped out, and looked Mark up and down.

Mark averted his eyes. He knew the rules. Kona was an elder and he would speak when he was spoken to.

"I have seen you in my dreams." Kona began.

"You search for your wife and son….. They are not here."

Mark starred at him in disbelief.

"What do you mean they aren't here?"

"They have gone into the desert with Seraphine."

"Why?" Mark snarled.

"Come inside." Kona said as he ducked to enter the tipi.

Inside, a fire burned. It felt good to warm up. The floor was covered in pelts.

Kona motioned for Mark to sit down.

"I need to find my family." Mark said sternly.

Kona motioned to the floor once again.

"You have much to learn on this journey."

He pointed to the pelts.

"Sit."

Mark reluctantly sat down. He didn't have time for this.

Kona sat opposite him. Mark starred at him, waiting for him to say something, but Kona seemed to be in no hurry.

A young girl entered the tipi bringing tow steaming bowls of food.

She handed Kona a bowl, and Mark next. He reluctantly took it.

"Look, I need to find …"

Kona cut him off in mid sentence.

"Eat."

Mark sighed and lifted the wooden spoon to his mouth. He was starving. It was the best meal he had eaten in a long time.

Mark ate quickly. Kona took his time, as he watched him impatiently.

The girl entered with a second bowl for Mark. He took this one willingly.

As he ate Kona began to speak.

"The dark devils have come to our lands. For many, many years they have diseased YOUR country. Now they have come into our lands, they have stolen and killed our children. Our women. I Have seen it.

I have seen the white giant, and the dark lady. Now she is something else. A dark spirit has come into her. A Kigatilik."

"What the hell is that?" Mark asked.

"It means you much harm. It will not rest until it has what it seeks."

He pulled a pipe out of a satchel, and lit the end.

He took a deep draw, and exhaled slowly.

"They want my wife and daughter for their cult." Mark stated.

Kona looked at him. He spoke slowly, deliberately.

"The cult you say. I don't know what you speak of. But the Kigatilik seeks the sun child.

She is dark, and seeks to sacrifice the one that comes from the light.

I have seen it in my visions. She had the sun child in her grasp, but another came, and flew away with the child. A Raven, sent down from the great Manitou himself."

Marks hair stood up on his arms as chills passed over him.

Kona starred into the fire.

"The Demon, as you call it in your world, cannot harm the ones marked with the seal of the Great Mannitou."

"You mean God?" Mark asked impatiently.

"You will play a small part in this. Your great role comes later."

His eyes fixated on the fire, he seemed to be in a trance, of some sort.

"There is another giant, this one not dark, but not much light, either. The sun child will fill him with new light. He will come, and if Manitou is in your favor he can bring down the dark lady." He sighed. "I cannot see the outcome."

"Where is my family", Mark asked quietly.

"They have gone to the Devils Bone. The place of the final battle, between light and dark."

Mark closed his eyes, and tried to control his breathing. He understood every part of what Kona was saying. As much as he hadn't wanted to believe in Seraphine, or in the electricity that he had felt, when Josephine touched him, he knew it to be true.

It was all real. Every part. He hadn't believed it until now.

"What can I do?" he asked.

"You will travel to the Devils Bone with Kona. You will play a part, but your Giant has a larger role to fill."

"Now you must rest, I am tired." Kona said quietly. Once again as if summoned the girl entered and handed Mark a cup, with a hot steaming liquid.

"Drink." He ordered.

"What is it?" Mark asked as he sipped the bitter liquid.

The old man ignored his question, and continued to talk.

"Kona has seen far ahead of this day. When the battle begins, you will be there."
Mark drank the warm liquid and in a matter of minutes, his eyes began to blur.

He leaned back against the pelts, and fell asleep. Kona watched over him and prayed to his god for strength.

The next morning the horses were packed and ready.

Mark, Kona and five warriors rode out towards the devils bone.

Grey woke up, and dressed quietly. The sun was just beginning to come up.

Raven slept soundly. He looked in on Josephine. As he walked away, he wondered if she had grown. Her legs seemed to reach the end of the playpen. She looked quietly around the room, as he walked out the door locking it behind him.

He jogged to the small restaurant, and ten minutes later, returned with coffee, and breakfast.

When he walked into the room, Josephine stood next to the table. He set down his packages, and sat down on the kitchen chair.

Josephine walked up to Grey and took his hand. Her eyes went blank as she watched his life unfold in her mind. He watched her, not sure what was happening.

He did not know that it played like a video in her head. She watched his family being slaughtered, and Grey fall to his knees, cursing God. Then there was only cold, and snow. Darkness and sorrow.

A tear fell onto her cheek. Her eyes met his.

"He has not forgotten you." The small voice said.

George helped the thing that was once Anita. It was unsteady, not used to being in a body. Abbadon had not possessed a human in a hundred years.

Stupid humans, didn't understand what they were chanting, and had summoned her.

George led the thing to the van. "Take me to the desert" it commanded.

This was bad. George didn't want to go, he had his own plans, but the thing eyed him suspiciously.

His contact would already be there, but it was too late. He could have stopped Anita and kept the prize for himself, but this thing was a whole other matter.

He would be lucky to keep his life.

Francis sat in the back with his priestess that was no longer human, a thought he could not comprehend. He watched the scenery go by, humming to himself.

George drove, to where the road ended. His thoughts raced. He hoped somehow it would still all work out in his favor.

Abbadon climbed out of the van on all fours and sniffed the ground.

"Yesssssss……" it hissed smelling the faint scent of Megan and Sam.

The days passed for Grey and Raven. She told him of her life, and he told her of his. They played with Josie when she was awake.

Josephine slept an unusual amount. She didn't appear to be sick. She ate when they fed her. He had a feeling she was stocking up her energy. He had pulled her playpen around the corner into the small kitchen, blocking out the light.

Grey felt like a different man. He hadn't thought about dying since they had left the compound. Somehow he had a reason to live.

He felt a little guilty because he could no longer picture Molly's face. It just wouldn't come to him. He pushed it out of his mind and tried not to dwell on it.

It had been ten years. He figured he had done his time. It was time to move on. Grey was ready. He had these feelings for Raven that he didn't understand. Things were happening.

He knew it should wait, until all this chaos was over, but the feelings would not wait. She was so familiar to him, like he had known her forever. The third day, as the baby slept, he confessed how he was feeling.

"I feel like I have known you forever. I don't understand it, but it's how I feel."

He took her small hand in his, starring down at it.

"I feel the same way." She whispered softly.

Greydon Stark took her face in his hands and kissed her gently. They kissed for a few minutes, when he pulled back. He didn't want to move too fast.

"Don't stop," she said.

"I don't want to freak you out, after the things you have been through."

"I don't know if I am going to live or die, and I am not wasting another minute of my life." He pulled her into his arms and kissed her a little harder with more passion. His heart pounded out of his chest.

Raven pulled his shirt over his head. He was scared. It sounded stupid. Grey wouldn't even say it out loud. He didn't have to.

"What's wrong", she said, when she saw the look on his face.

"I..." he stammered.

"It's ok." She touched his face. She knew there had been no one since his wife. He had confessed that the woman he visited in town, was a decoy, and all they had ever done was play scrabble.

"We don't have time to waste. I have these feelings for you, that I can't explain. I think I love you." Raven said.

That was all he needed to hear. He pulled her into his lap, pulling her shirt off.

Grey kissed her neck and face and slowly ran his hands over her back and shoulders and her breasts. He lay her down on the bed and inched her pants off. He wanted her so bad. He kissed her again, and again.

He was trying to control himself and take is time. Grey stood and dropped his pants. He watched her eyes widen as she starred at his manhood. He felt himself blush. He was well proportioned, to say the least.

Grey saw the look on her face.

"Are you ok?" he whispered.

"Yes." She lied, as he waited for the truth.

"I am a little scared. She admitted."

"Don't be." Grey replied, as he pulled her hips down to the edge of the bed, where he kneeled. He kissed her inner thighs, as his hand moved between her legs. When she moaned in pleasure he moved between her legs and let his tongue do the work.

He licked and flicked his tongue around until she writhed with pleasure.

He sat up and slowly moved next to her. Raven was breathing hard, her head thrown back in pleasure. She looked up at him as he moved on top of her. He legs went around him instinctively, as he entered her slowly, carefully. He closed his eyes, as a moan escaped his lips. It had been a long time...and never like this. He moved slowly leaning down to kiss her. His hips continued to thrust slowly, as Grey made love to her.

Much later, once he knew she had come two or three times, he let himself go, careful not to hurt her. He kissed her, and rolled onto his side, pulling her into his arms.

"I think I love you too." He whispered.

During the night he made love to her again. He couldn't get enough of her. Grey had been crazy about her since he met her.

Greys phone rang just after daylight. It was Tom.

He answered suspiciously.

"Where you been dude?"

"I've been shot. I need help." He sounded muffled and far away.

"Where are you?" The road he was parked on was only thirty minutes from Grey.

He wasn't sure. It could be a trap. He rubbed his face.

He looked over at Josephine.

"Well?"

She cocked her head to the side, then nodded.

Grey gave Tom directions, to the diner down the street, just to be sure.

When the black Dodge pulled up, Grey was sitting in the booth. He spotted Tom.

He watched for a moment as the door opened, and watched Tom stagger out.

He ran out to help him up.

"Shit, what happened?"

"I told you I got shot. The CIA wants to shut me up. They don't want another scandal. There is a governor from Texas involved and his brother, more old southern money."

Grey helped him into the passenger side, after checking out the rest of the vehicle.

Once they pulled up at the small efficiency, he helped him inside.

"You sure your car ain't got a bug?" Grey asked.

"I know it doesn't. I stole it."

"Well, Mr. Law man, looks like you're in for good now." He joked.

Grey went outside and pulled the SUV around back.

He came inside, and cleaned Tom's wound with the water Raven had boiled.

Grey leaned over him, with the tweezers.

"This might sting a little bit."

"MOTHER FUCKER" Tom yelled, as Grey dug the bullet out of his gut.

"Watch your mouth." Grey scolded, glancing over at Josephine.

Grey washed his hands, after Tom was bandaged up.

Josephine walked over and pointed at Greys pocket.

"What?" he asked.

At that moment the panic button he had given Megan went off.

"We gotta go." He said. He was already on his feet throwing his clothes and guns in the duffle bag.

Raven packed quickly.

They helped Tom into the SUV, and headed towards the reservation.

"My momma needs help." The color had drained out of her face. She knew what was coming.

"Did she just speak?" Raven asked.

"Yes" Grey said.

"It's coming." Josie whispered.

"What?" Grey asked.

"What is coming?" He asked again, sternly.

"Abbadon." She said quietly, then hiding her face in Ravens side.

Tom sat up, in the back seat.

"Who the hell is that?"

He pulled out his phone and googled the name.

"All there is, is some devil stuff." Tom said.

"Read it." Grey commanded.

"It says as a human Abbadon was handpicked by Lucifer himself and turned into a demon by Cain, then she became one of the knights of hell, possessing souls and causing mass destruction and death."

"What is this?" Tom said.

"Has she possessed someone?" Raven asked Josephine.

"Yes." She answered.

"Who?" Raven whispered, fearing she knew the answer.

"Anita." The child replied.

They drove to the cabin, and picked up the trailor, with the two four wheelers.

Ten minutes later they were heading into the desert. Grey and Josephine on one, and Raven and Tom on the other. Three hours later, they reached the oasis.

It was abandoned. The sand was too thick to continue on the four wheelers. They drank from the abandoned water hole and sat down to rest for a few moments.

Josephine pointed west. Grey rounded up two of the abandoned horses, and they headed out, once again, unsure of their future, or what it would bring.

They were all relying on the words of a three year old. Grey tried not to think about it too much. He felt like he just needed to believe.

The horses trudged on. Grey met Ravens eyes on several occasions, and mouthed "I love you," to her. He of all people knew to say what he meant, and that there may not be a second chance. He was not dwelling in the past, but being realistic. If this Demon was chasing them, he had no idea how to kill it, or if any of them would even survive it. He prayed that they would. For the first time in a long time he wanted to live. Grey felt like he had been given a second chance at life, and at love. He would never take it for granted again.

It was true when Josephine had taken his hand and told him that God hadn't forgotten him, it changed something inside of him.

He felt like he was not alone anymore and no matter what happened it would be ok. Grey was on the course that he needed to be on. He was brought here. Not by chance, but by fate, on a predestined course.

Grey had a strong feeling that the fate of the world depended on this child. He watched her as she rode in silence. From time to time she opened her eyes and looked at him, as if she knew what he was thinking.

Just her glances gave him renewed hope. He believed her, even though he didn't understand all of it just yet.

He was willing to fight for her, and for his friends, no matter what.

Mark saw the outline of the cave come into view. He looked over at Kona, who had stopped his pony and dismounted.

He was old, yet he moved very quickly. By the time Mark dismounted he was standing directly in front of him.

He pulled something wrapped in a cloth from his pouch, and offered it to Mark.

"What is this?"

"Open it." Kona said quietly.

Mark unwrapped the soft cloth, and pulled out a long silver triple edged dagger.

It glinted in the sunlight. At the cross section of the blade, a three pointed star.

He looked at Kona, questioningly.

"An Angel Blade. It is the only thing that will kill her."

"Who?"

"The beast that comes for all of you."

"Abbadon."

"You must call her by name, and then use the blade, either in her neck, or heart." He stated.

"It is the only way."

Mark shook his head, in disbelief, and stared down at the blade. A sudden flash made him cover his eyes.

When he looked up Kona was gone, and he was alone. Six horses stood where the men had been.

Mark didn't know what was going on, or what was coming. It was unbelievable.

All he knew was he had to find his family, and he was ready to kill whatever came his way.

Abbadon moved on all fours across the sand. Her entire body seemed to move at once. She glided across the sand stopping to sniff the ground every few minutes, to ensure she was still on the trail.

It gave George and Francis a chance to catch up. George was sweating profusely. He didn't know how much further he could go.

He thought of making a run for it. As if the thing could read his mind it sneered in his direction. He thought better of it. Above everything else, he wanted to live. George liked his life.

He shook his head. This was surreal. He pulled his knees up to his chest, starring at the creature that had once been Anita. He guessed the ascension was no longer necessary.

Suddenly the creature looked up and moved on. He stood and followed behind her. Francis fell further and further behind. He yelled for George to wait, but got no response.

Finally exhausted, he lay down on the sand. He watched the sky as it clouded over. He didn't understand anything that was happening. He just wanted to kill Megan. The priestess had promised him. Suddenly a man stood over him.

He sat up and scooted backwards on his bottom.

Kona watched him closely.

"What do you want?" Francis asked.

Kona took his hand and whispered something into the wind.

His voice growing louder and louder as it blended with the sound of the storm that was brewing. The Albino bowed his head, as the wind and sand blew around them.

Mark tucked the blade in the back of his pants, and started up the hill. The cave came into view.

He took a deep breath and crept inside, expecting the worst.

Megan sat on the ground holding Sam, who was asleep. Her feet were tied.

Lupe, and Seraphine sat beside her. Their feet also tied.

Redbird stood in front of them with his back to Mark.

He breathed a sigh of relief that they were both alive.

"Why do you do this, uncle?" Lupe's distressed voice stated.

"I had no choice. I traded a life for a life."

"You are a coward." Seraphine said.

"Don't you want Lupe to live?" he cried.

"Yes, I want her to live, but not at the expense of another. There are other ways."

"No this is the only way. Her life for Lupe's." he said pointing at Megan.

George had made it very clear. He would keep coming. Redbird had seen some of his handi work when he had been on scene with the tribal police.

There would be no stopping him.

"Let my son go. Seraphine, you take him. If you save my son I will go willingly."

"No," He stated coldly. "I cannot. We wait."

Redbird was getting nervous. George should have been here hours ago.

Mark took the 9mm out of his pants, and cocked it, when he felt a hand on his shoulder.

He spun around to see Josephine standing beside him.

"Not yet," she whispered.

He backed out of the entryway and followed her down the hill, out of sight.

He saw Grey, Raven, and Tom, waiting.

"Are you out of your FUCKING mind bringing her here?" Mark hissed.

"I didn't..... She brought us." Grey said somberly.

Mark stared at his daughter, quizzically.

He quickly filled them in on Redbird conspiring with George.

"We have bigger problems." Grey said.

"What." Mark stated.

"I don't know if you're going to believe me."

"Just tell him." Raven demanded.

Grey told Mark of the demon that hunted them. When he was done Mark starred at him. He shook his head in disbelief. Running his fingers through his hair. How could this be. It was exactly what Kona had said.

"You have all gone crazy. It can't be. This is something straight out of a horror movie." Mark argued with himself.

He continued to shake his head.

"Take my daughter out of here." He demanded.

"NO." the voice was louder than anyone had ever heard it.

All eyes were on Josephine as she spoke. "We must all be here, to defeat her."

"Why?" he asked.

"We have the Mark." She turned and lifted her hair. Showing him the birthmark.

He starred at the star, And suddenly he knew it was true.

"What does it mean?" he asked. Still in shock that she was talking at all, and that he was having a full grown conversation with a three year old.

"She is coming for all of us. There are three of us with the Mark. She can only kill us, if we are all together."

"Then I will hide you." He said frantically.

"No, I cannot hide. You can only defeat her if the three stars come together."

"Who else has the mark?" He believed. As impossible as it was.

"Sam." The child said.

"You said there were three. Is it your mother?"

"No."

"Who else?" he pressed.

Josephine pointed at Raven.

Mark lifted her hair and saw the small birthmark, the three point Star.

It was the same as the one on the dagger.

"You said three stars. Yours is not the same."

"I am not the third." She said quietly, smiling.

"But you have a mark."

She walked up to him, and touched his cheeks with both hands.

"I am the sun child." He was filled with an Indescribable feeling, of peace and love.

"I am the alpha and the omega." The small voice said.

"The resurrection, all that is good in this world, and above.

I am sent by my father, my heavenly father. I am the sun child....You are the third star."

www.ingramcontent.com/pod-product-compliance
Lightning Source LLC
Chambersburg PA
CBHW080843250626
47163CB00004B/431